"Sam? Oh, my G   that you?"

"Great," he muttered, "the crazy woman in my tree knows my name."

Nicole pushed away from the trunk and started down with the use of the rope.

"I wouldn't use that rope," he said and moved closer.

"Why not? It got me up here." Her skirt blew in the breeze and he caught a glimpse of her long legs.

"Because it might—"

Before he could finish the sentence, the rope snapped in two. He rushed forward and grabbed the woman around the waist to stop her from falling to the ground. Her back pressed into his front. Her hair smelled floral and like expensive perfume with rich undertones. It made him want to lean down and draw in more of the scent.

He set her down in front of him. She spun immediately and pressed the length of her body against him and hugged him around the neck, pulling him down to her height. She was at least a foot shorter than him. Even if she was crazy, his body responded to the soft curves pressed into his hardness.

"I can't believe it's you."

HIS SMALL-TOWN SWEETHEART

BY
AMANDA BERRY

Published in Great Britain 2015
by Mills & Boon, an imprint of Harlequin (UK) Limited,
Eton House, 18-24 Paradise Road, Richmond, Surrey, TW9 1SR

© 2015 Amanda Berry

ISBN: 978-0-263-25113-5

23-0215

Harlequin (UK) Limited's policy is to use papers that are natural, renewable and recyclable products and made from wood grown in sustainable forests. The logging and manufacturing processes conform to the legal environmental regulations of the country of origin.

Printed and bound in Spain
by CPI, Barcelona

Between walking her Jack Russell-beagle mix, petting her two cats and driving her two kids all over creation, **Amanda Berry** writes contemporary romance novels (thanks to a supportive husband). A Midwest girl stuck in the wetlands of South Carolina, she finds inspiration in her small-town upbringing. A list of her current releases and backlist can be found at amanda-berry.com.

To my Little Man and Lady Jane.
When your path is dark know that at the end of it there
is light. You two are my light.

Chapter One

At least I'm on the right side of the grass. Better on top than below. Nicole Baxter stood in the last place she'd ever thought she'd end up—the front porch of a farm she hadn't been to in seventeen years. The fields were lush from the months of spring rain they had received. Even the stifling heat of the Illinois summer hadn't diminished the crops. With fall approaching, it wouldn't be long before the fields were stripped of their bounty.

"You all settled in your room?" Her father, John Baxter, joined her on the porch.

"Yes." She smiled up at him and shifted on her high heels. Probably the last time she'd wear them for a while. "Thanks again for letting me stay here. I swear I'll only be here for a few weeks. A month, tops. Just until I get back on my feet again."

"This is your home. You stay as long as you like." His

gaze followed the combine out in the western field. Her twin brothers, Ethan and Wes, were out there working.

"Thanks." She could argue with him, insist that she wasn't used to taking charity. That this hadn't been her home in a long time. That this was only a temporary setback. A few weeks in the uncomplicated town of Tawnee Valley would help her heal from her breakup and find a new job that was ten times better than the one that had been eliminated.

"I think I'll take a walk." Nicole stretched her arms over her head and let the heat of the sun melt away her worries. It was only her first day back, and she couldn't imagine spending it inside, searching the internet for a job. It wasn't as if she didn't have time on her hands.

"In those things?" Her father looked skeptically at her three-inch heels.

"I won't go far. Besides, the ground isn't that soft." She flashed him a cheeky grin. "And they match my outfit."

"You're going to do what you are going to do, no matter what I say." Her dad shook his head.

She kissed him on the cheek and stepped off the porch. As she reached the fence gate, she turned and waved at him. Her floral skirt swirled around her knees. While inside the house, her bag was a mess. She'd packed in a few hours, desperate to get out of the apartment she'd shared with Jeremy. Seven years down the toilet because they weren't "connecting" anymore. Whatever that meant.

It was going to take her a few hours to unpack in her old bedroom. But she was through waiting for stuff. She'd waited for Jeremy's proposal. She'd waited for a promotion. The only things waiting had gotten her were no boyfriend and no job. And not enough money to stay in LA.

As she walked far enough away that the house disappeared behind a hill, she took in a full breath and spun in a circle. Seventeen years and she still felt most at home here, where she'd played as a child. After her parents divorced when she was fourteen, her mother had taken her to LA, and the twins had stayed with Dad.

Even though this path was a little overgrown now, she followed it, just as she'd traveled it almost every day until she was fourteen.

Best days of her life. She wanted to recapture that time and forget all the crap that came after. Deep in the wooded part of their land, right where it abutted the Ward farm, was where she and her best friend would meet. She headed toward the tree, hoping their creation was still there.

When her heel sank into the ground slightly, she stopped and pulled off her shoes. Her toes curled into the damp grass. It felt wonderful, liberating. How long had it been since her feet had been in grass? As she approached the fence, she looked around. Didn't her father say that Sam Ward was in charge of the farm now?

A little thrill went through her heart. She went to the post where it was easiest to climb the fence. It wasn't as easy as when she was a kid, but she got over and wouldn't be embarrassed if someone saw her do it with her skirt hitched up over her knees. Back then, she'd worn jeans or shorts and a T-shirt that might or might not have been washed since the last time she wore it. Her mother had put her hair into two braids to keep it from getting too tangled. She'd always come home wearing more mud than a hog trying to get cool in the summer heat. Band-Aids covered her knees. Her nails were broken and dirty. A happy little mess.

Now her nails were perfectly manicured. Her knees were smooth and clean with only a few scars from her childhood adventures. Her dark hair flowed over her shoulders, tangle-free with the right products and a straightening iron. Her skirt and blouse were feminine with flowers, the way Jeremy had always liked her to dress. Maybe she should go shopping…

As she rounded a bend, she saw it. After all these years, it was still there. The slab of wood they'd built up in the tree and called a tree house. She stopped in front of the tree and dropped her shoes to the ground. Glancing around and seeing no one, she smiled and grabbed the rope.

Sam Ward had never minded chores, but he was getting tired of finding damaged fencing along his property borders. John Baxter was usually good about it; if he found it first, he fixed it. But the new guy who'd bought the place to the south loved to drive his four-wheeler in his fields, but not actually keep up the fencing or anything else.

As Sam walked the fence bordering the Baxter property, Barnabus, his big, shaggy dog, trailed along behind him. Suddenly Barnabus lifted his head and gave a sharp bark before trotting into the woods.

Sam whistled, but the dog kept going. Probably a squirrel or something, but it could be a larger injured animal. He had sheep in the field at this time of year, but even a squirrel would be a welcome interruption into the monotony his life had become. Since his recovery from his valve surgery, he had been feeling ten times better than earlier this spring, prior to the operation. The tedium hadn't bothered him before, but now he felt as if he'd been wasting his life out here all these years. Some days he wished he could just move away and start over. But this was his family's farm, passed down to him by his parents.

A flash of white in a tree caught his attention. He quickened his pace down the old trail. If that new neighbor was littering on his land, he'd need to have a talk with him. But as he got closer, what Sam saw in the tree made no sense.

A slender young woman in a floral skirt and blouse stood on the platform that had once been his tree house. Her black hair lifted and floated on the wind. As he drew closer, he noticed the high heels at the base of the tree.

"You're trespassing," he called up to the clearly insane woman in his tree.

"No, I'm not. I built this place with my own two hands." She turned and leaned forward against a thick offshoot of the trunk. She had the smile of a garden fairy, full of mischief. He couldn't tell her eye color from so far away, but he could tell her eyes were light.

"I built that tree house almost twenty years ago." He squinted as the sun moved to shine into his eyes.

"Sam?" Her voice sounded incredulous. "Oh, my God. Sam Ward, is that you?"

"Great," he muttered, "the crazy woman in my tree knows my name."

She pushed away from the trunk and started down with the use of the rope.

"I wouldn't use that rope," he said and moved closer.

"Why not? It got me up here." Her skirt blew in the

breeze and he caught a glimpse of her long legs and pink boy-short underwear before he could look away.

"Because it might—"

Before he could finish the sentence, the rope snapped in two. He rushed forward and grabbed the woman around the waist to stop her from falling to the ground. Her back pressed into his front. Her hair smelled floral and like expensive perfume with rich undertones, making him want to lean into her and draw in more of the scent.

He set her down in front of him. She spun immediately and pressed the length of her body against him and hugged him around the neck, pulling him down to her height. She was at least a half foot shorter than him. Even if she was crazy, his body responded to the soft curves pressed into his hardness.

"I can't believe it's you," she said. Her tone made it seem as if she was ecstatic to see him. No one was that happy to see him. She must be certifiable.

She finally pulled away. Maybe she'd finally noticed he wasn't holding in return. "Sam, it's me."

He looked into the crazy lady's light green eyes. Surrounded by her dark lashes, the green reminded him of spring and new growth.

"You don't know who I am, do you?" She smiled, and her eyes sparkled. Her lips drew his attention.

Aware of how close they were standing, he took a step back. "Should I?"

"Are you scared I'll give you cooties or something?" She laughed, and it tickled the air around his ears pleasantly. "I cross my heart and hope to die that I have not been infected."

When she crossed her heart with her finger, his gaze

took in her breasts and waist and hips. By the time he lifted his eyes to hers, she had her eyebrow raised and was watching him with such an intensity that a spark of awareness flowed through him.

"Oh, I think he might have it, folks," she said in a game show–style voice. "Come on. You never were as fast as I was, but I thought since you grew up so damned tall… When did you get that tall?"

"Nikki?" He couldn't keep the awe from his voice. The corners of his mouth twitched into a quick smile. This couldn't be the same tomboy with hair falling out of her braids and dirty jeans. She'd been straight as a rail and proud of it.

She grinned. "I go by Nicole now. Mom thought it sounded more mature, and who was I to argue with her?"

"You left."

"All right. Apparently it's going to take you some time to catch up. Yes, my mom and I moved to California when I was fourteen after the divorce. I'm back now. Staying with Dad until I can get back on my feet."

"Are you sick?" He took a partial step forward, searching for signs of sickness. His own brush with illness was still a fresh wound, though he was almost completely healed.

Her brow furrowed and she shrugged. "No, just having issues with life in general."

He rubbed his hand over the back of his neck. His brain was still trying to reconcile the beautiful woman in front of him with the rough-and-tumble tomboy best friend he used to know. "What were you doing in the tree?"

She swung around and looked up into the tree. "I wondered if I could still climb it."

"In a dress?"

She looked at him over her shoulder and smiled. "It's a skirt. I didn't think anyone would be out in the field at this time of day. I just remember how many days we spent up there and wondered if I could feel that way again."

"What way?" He squinted up at the old tree house. "Dirty with splinters in your feet?"

Her laughter made his gut tighten. He wasn't sure if he wanted to hear it more, or not at all. It made him feel strange.

"Maybe," she said before she turned back to him and closed the distance between them until her toes were only a few inches from his boots. She put a hand on top of her head and moved her hand toward his chest. "How did you get so tall? We were the same height when I left."

"I grew."

Her hand reached out and touched his arm lightly. He automatically flexed his muscles beneath her touch.

Her green eyes looked up at him with a twinkle in them. "You certainly did. Do you spend all your time bench-pressing cattle?"

The image struck him as funny, and a slight laugh, more like a release of air, escaped before he could stop it.

"Did you lose your funny bone, too?" She squeezed his elbow. "Nope, it feels like one is still in there."

His lips tried to curve up again. She was something else. He didn't know what to say, so, as usual, he remained silent, trying to figure out this situation.

She breathed in deeply and wrapped her arms around his waist again, resting her head against his chest. "It is so good to see you again. I was afraid you'd changed too much, or that, once I saw you, I wouldn't recognize you, but here you are. Oh, my goodness, we always had so much fun together. Climbing trees, running through the fields, snowball fights."

She squeezed him slightly. He held his breath, willing his body not to respond to the temptation of her pressed against him. It was only a friendly hug. It didn't mean anything. Certainly not what the lower half of his body wanted it to mean. He shouldn't be thinking about her that way at all. This was Nikki. His best friend who left when he was fourteen, barely a teenager.

"Maybe I should take up cow lifting." She stayed cuddled against him. "I could definitely use some definition in my arms. But then that would be a lot of work and someone would have to spot me, because I can't lift a cow on my own."

As she leaned against him, he didn't know what to do with his arms. The top of her head almost reached his chin.

She lifted her head and looked up at him. "Would you spot me?"

With her this close, he could lift her the few inches he needed to be able to kiss her pretty pink lips. Would she taste as rich and darkly seductive as she smelled? Or would she taste like the spring her eyes promised? Strawberries and mint.

"Sam?" Her smile kept his eyes glued to her lips. "Would you spot me?"

Her words made no sense. He shook himself and lifted his gaze to her smiling eyes. "What?"

"In cow lifting? You would definitely keep a cow from falling on me. Wouldn't you?"

"What?" Apparently she'd lost a few marbles in California.

She released him, and the lack of her warmth hit him the wrong way. "I guess you're right, cow lifting isn't for me. I'm sure there are other things that could help me improve my figure while I'm here."

She bent down and picked up her shoes.

"You don't have to improve your figure." The words slipped out.

"Thanks." Her cheeks flushed pink. "You always were sweet. I can't wait to see what you've done with the house and the farm. Did you keep those rocks we collected? The ones that had the crystal-like appearance?"

"From the creek? Yeah."

She was like a whirlwind that he had no chance of escaping or keeping up with. A very unintentionally sexy whirlwind. When they were younger, there'd never been anything but friendship between them. More often than not, she'd beat him at racing. Now the only thing racing was his heart; if it weren't for the attraction pulsing through his veins, he'd be worried that another fainting episode was about to happen.

"So what are you doing in the woods at this time of day? Searching for fairies and dragons? The twins are out in the field, joyriding."

Her smile was a constant that he was beginning to appreciate. People didn't smile at him this much. As soon as he opened his mouth and said something, they generally stopped smiling. He didn't mind keeping his distance from folks. It made things easier.

"Checking the fence." He put his hands in his pockets and looked back toward the fence.

"I'd offer to come with you, but—" she held up her shoes "—I haven't quite reacclimated to farm life. Can you believe this is what I've been wearing since I left here?" She pulled her skirt out to the side. The sunlight made the thin material almost transparent.

He swallowed the lump that had formed in his throat at the remembrance of what was under that skirt. "It's nice."

"Thanks, but it isn't really right for strolling through the fields. I just couldn't help myself. I didn't want to wait to find the right clothes or shoes to come out here. It's been too long."

He stepped back to discourage her from hugging him again.

"We really need to get together. I left the house without even grabbing my phone." She laughed. "It's been ages since I've left it behind without worrying that I'd miss something from work. Do you know what I mean?"

He shrugged. His brothers had bought him a cell phone and made him promise to keep it on him because of his condition. It was in the bottom of a drawer somewhere. He wasn't sure if it was even charged currently. "I have to get back to work."

"Of course, but I'm holding you to going out with me for a beer, or maybe I'll wander over with a six-pack, so we can catch up on the past seventeen years."

He nodded and whistled for Barnabus, who had wandered off while they'd been talking.

She closed the distance between them again and wrapped herself around him for the third time. "I'm glad I ran into you."

He awkwardly patted her back this time. His body felt charged with electricity everywhere she touched him. He stared down at her dark hair. She wasn't like the women in town who tried to draw his attention. Most of those women were divorced or widowed. He didn't have a problem with them, but he wasn't sure he was the best choice for a long-term relationship, which is what at least some of those women had wanted. As long as he picked the right ones, things worked out just fine.

But Nicole had been his buddy. Her father, John, would kill him if he messed with her; besides, they'd never been like that. They'd gone frogging together back when she wore braids and T-shirts and walked like a boy.

There was nothing boy-like about her now, except those underwear that he shouldn't be thinking about. He wouldn't even know about the different styles of underwear if he hadn't been forced to go back-to-school shopping with his sister-in-law and niece. The only reason they apparently had taken him was to get him out of the house more often.

Nicole would be better off if she didn't get to know the guy he'd become and just remembered the boy she'd left behind.

She released him, graced him with another smile and spun in a circle. "I feel better already. See you soon, Sam."

As she sashayed away from him toward the fence, his eyes were drawn to the curve of her bottom. If she was enticing in a skirt, she'd be irresistible in a pair of jeans. Barnabus rushed out of the bushes and sat patiently at his feet. This summer had just gotten interesting.

Chapter Two

Nicole straightened her shirt, tucked her hair behind her ear and shifted the six-pack from one hand to the other. She stood in front of Sam's screen door, which he could walk by any minute and see her standing out here in the dark like a ninny. This was Sam. Her friend, her confidant.

Taking a deep breath, she knocked on the door. She could hear some shuffling from the other room, and then he was walking toward her. Holy crap, it hadn't just been her imagination. He was tall, dark and handsome. Not at all the kid she'd left behind.

Earlier today, his blue eyes had been amazing close-up, sparkling in the sunlight with flecks of dark blue mingled with light blue and even hints of gold. Not that she'd been staring earlier. It had taken most of her willpower not to check him out the way he'd done to her. Farming had definitely been good for his development. His chest was broad. His arms were muscular, but not overly so. And she'd bet money that he was packing his own six-pack under that AC/DC T-shirt.

As he drew closer, he ran his hand through his thick, shaggy hair and she wanted to do the same, except, in her fantasy, when she wove her fingers in his hair, she would jerk his full lips down to hers. When he stopped at the door, she held up the six-pack and smiled.

She needed to stop thinking of Sam as eye candy. Their meeting today had caught her off guard. She hadn't thought, just reacted. And it had felt good.

With everything that had happened in her life recently, she could really use a friend. Maybe Sam could use a friend, too. She'd kept his friendship close to her heart when she'd moved to California. Sam, who'd always known the right thing to do. She'd written him letters as she maneuvered through a new school and social situations she never would have experienced in Tawnee Valley. She'd never sent the letters that shared all her secrets and fears. Just a few when she'd first moved away. Right now, she needed a friend more than sex… At least, that's what she reminded herself of when he stood on the other side of the door looking like sex on a stick.

He opened the screen door, and she slid through the opening under his arm, into the kitchen, before he could tell her not to.

"How's it going? I brought beer." She moved around him, catching hints of the crispness of his soap and that distinct, manly scent that was all Sam. Raw, powerful.

"You aren't going to hug me again, are you?" He eyed her suspiciously.

She shrugged and set the beer on the table. "Probably."

She pulled out two beers and handed him one. He took it from her, almost as if he were afraid to touch her. He hadn't returned her hugs earlier. Of course, he hadn't been touchy-feely when he was a fourteen-year-old, either.

Twisting off the cap to her beer, she glanced around the kitchen. It looked the same. Her dad had mentioned that Mr. and Mrs. Ward had died years ago. Other than that, her father hadn't talked much about the Wards, except to say Sam was a hard worker.

"Cheers," she said and clinked her bottle against his. They both took a swig and then stood there awkwardly with their beers. "So...does the rest of the house look the same? The kitchen definitely hasn't changed."

He shrugged. His gaze dipped down to her bare legs. She'd changed into shorts and had managed to find her one pair of sneakers that she didn't use for running.

"This is ridiculous," she said.

He lifted his gaze to hers and raised his eyebrow.

"We were once best friends, Sam. I used to sleep in your bed. We used to run around in bathing suits and sneakers. I showed you mine and you showed me yours...in a perfectly scientific discovery sense. We should be able to have a beer together and catch up like normal people."

He shifted his weight on his feet, and the corner of his mouth twitched upward, about as much of a smile as he could make, apparently. "Sure. You want to see the house?"

"I'd love to." That had been what she was angling for, after all.

Sam had a house, a job, a couple of dogs that had greeted her when she walked up, while she was adrift in life. She didn't have a job and could end up anywhere in the United States with her search. She'd just left a long-term relationship and wasn't in the right frame of mind to start anything. Even with her old best friend who was now hot but completely anchored to this town.

He led the way, and she noted how he filled out his carpenter jeans with a very nicely shaped butt. As he stopped abruptly, she ran into him. He looked over his shoulder at her with that disgruntled expression of his.

"Do you ever smile?" She returned his look before she stepped back and glanced around the dining room. "Nothing's changed. How do you manage that? I'm constantly changing things. Moving furniture, painting walls, buying lamps. Jeremy used to complain that I couldn't leave anything for longer than a minute."

"Who's Jeremy?" he said in that gruff voice of his. Definitely lower toned, it made her spine tingle in response. Could she get him to read her a book or even the dictionary? Maybe the ingredients off a cereal box? Whole grain oats, sugar, calcium carbonate...

"My ex-boyfriend." She wished she could say "my dog" or maybe "my snake," but he was her ex. "We lived together in LA. He got the apartment. I lost my job and came back here."

"That sucks." He led her into the living room. There was a nice flat-screen and a game console, along with a few recliners and a couch that had seen better days. He gestured to one of the chairs and sat in the one with the best view of the TV. His chair looked like the most lived-in one.

"It did suck, but it was probably for the best." Jeremy

had actually had the gall to blame her parents' divorce as one of the reasons she wouldn't connect with him. It was ridiculous. "I don't want to think about it. I want to find out what you've been doing since I last saw you. You obviously didn't complete our tree house."

He shrugged. "Didn't have time."

Getting him to talk was like pulling teeth. They used to talk over each other. They'd had so much to say and share. "I heard about your mom and dad. I was sorry I couldn't be here for you."

He nodded and looked at the label on his beer. The way his shoulders hunched told her he wasn't over the pain of losing them. She wanted to let him know that he could cry on her shoulder if he wanted. She wished she could have been there. As she'd been there for him when his dog died when they were eleven.

"You had to take care of Luke and Brady and the farm? That must have been tough. I couldn't imagine being responsible for another person at eighteen. I was barely responsible for myself. We won't discuss my poor goldfish burial ground. How did you date or go out?"

"I didn't."

She opened her mouth and snapped it shut. Someone as handsome as Sam didn't stay single without effort. He was gorgeous and tall, and she really wanted to see the solid body she'd hugged earlier. "Didn't you have a girlfriend in high school? I tried to date in high school, but the guys were always after one thing."

She looked at him, expecting his answer to her question. He was still looking at his beer label, lost in his own world.

"What?" He finally raised his gaze to hers.

"High school girlfriend?"

"Yeah, I had a few of those."

She took a drink of beer. "What about after high school? Anyone special?"

"No."

She felt compelled to fill the empty space around them. "Jeremy and I met in college. I think that's why we stayed together so long. I'm surprised you didn't have anyone like that. I mean, I realize you were busy with your brothers and the farm, but it's really hard to go for a long period without…well, you know. I mean, even in a relationship, you can have dry spells. We had been in a rut for a while. Maybe that was part of the problem. How long has it been for you?"

He lifted his eyebrows at her and she flushed with heat, realizing she'd just asked him how long it had been since he'd last had sex.

"Sorry. I tend to just say whatever's on my mind. My mom tried to stop me, but I like being honest and open. I can't stand when people keep secrets or don't say what's *really* on their minds. You were always honest with me. But I overstep boundaries all the time." She took a drink to stop herself from talking.

"My family says I don't talk enough." He returned to his perusal of his beer bottle.

She smiled. This was easy ground to tread upon. "How are your brothers?"

"Brady's married to Maggie Brown. They've got a kid, Amber. She's cool. Luke and Penny Montgomery are together down in St. Louis." He didn't lift his gaze to hers. His tone was matter-of-fact, just reciting facts with no emotion connected to them.

"That's exciting." The names of the women sounded somewhat familiar, but that wasn't what she was focused on. Had he really changed that much? The boy she used to know seemed to have turned into a crotchety old man at the age of thirty-one. Surely there was something exciting in his life. Maybe a hope or a dream or a wish for someone special to share his life with. She stood up and circled the room, looking at the pictures and knickknacks. They were all old with a coat of dust on them. Like his mother had placed them there and no one had moved them since. "You out here by yourself, then? No one special now?"

"No."

She stopped in front of the TV and turned to face him. Raising an eyebrow, she asked, "No, you aren't by yourself, or there's no one special?"

He lifted his gaze to hers, and she caught her breath at the deep blue of his eyes. They seemed empty of that spark he'd had when they ran through the yards with pretend weapons.

"No one," he said with all the emotion of a stone.

Even so, her heart fluttered in her chest. Nicole was hopelessly hopeful, as her mother would say. She crossed the room to stand in front of him. "So we're in the same boat, then. Single and alone with no one to worry about but ourselves."

"I guess so." He took a drink.

She glanced out the window at the accumulating darkness. Did that mean he wasn't interested in her? Or anyone? Did she want him to be interested in her? She might have had the teeny tiniest of small crushes on him in eighth grade, but nothing she ever would have acted on. They'd been best friends. Buds.

Gah. She needed to get out of her head. "I haven't seen good stars in ages. With the city lights and air pollution in LA, I was lucky to see a few stars in the Big Dipper. Do you remember when we used to wait until dark and look at the stars?"

He nodded, and a corner of his lips quirked up a little. That was all the encouragement she needed.

"Why don't we grab the rest of the beers and go see the stars? We can go down to the tree house and lie on our backs, look up at the stars, watch for falling stars." She grabbed his free hand and tugged on him. "Come on, Sam. Live a little."

His hand closed around hers. The feel of his firm grip shot through her and made her aware of his heat and how close she'd gotten to him. She was practically standing between his knees.

"Slow down, Nikki. Not everything has to be go, go, go." This time, when the corner of his mouth went up, a small dimple flashed at her.

She stopped tugging. The warmth of his hand spread through her. Her heart thrummed a steady rhythm as she thought of all the places she wanted that hand. Her eyes focused on his lips. She forced herself to focus on renewing their friendship. Clearing her mind and her throat, she said, "We could see the stars and watch the moon play hide-and-seek in the leaves of the tree. It'll be fun."

For a moment, she was sure he was going to turn her down. Instead, he stood. She didn't have time to back up. His heat surrounded her. It slipped through her clothes and wrapped itself tight around her lungs, making it hard to draw in a breath.

She ducked her head and stepped back until she could breathe again. She wanted only friendship from Sam. She was too screwed up to try anything else. Focusing on friendship should work. Just because she was attracted to him and maybe he thought she was attractive didn't mean she wanted to ruin what could be a good friendship for some meaningless sex.

The whole reason for coming to Tawnee Valley was to uncomplicate her life and figure out her next move. Sam could be a huge complication if she let things go that way. She wanted his steady presence to help guide her in the right direction, as he had when they were kids. And, yes, they had been children at the time and were now adults with a lot more complications, but that didn't have to stop them from being friends again. Guys and girls could be friends.

When Nicole wasn't touching him, Sam could think straight. They grabbed a couple of flashlights and the beer and headed into the fields. Barnabus and Rebel, Barnabus's puppy, who was almost a year old, followed them. Sam had promised himself that he was going to allow himself to live, even if he couldn't leave his family's farm.

Following Nicole wouldn't hurt anything. He was curious what had happened to her after she left Tawnee Valley. In the early years after her departure, he'd started letters to her but never finished them. Time had been against him with school and chores. Then so much time had passed that it seemed strange to write to a girl who had once been his friend.

"With the rope gone, how are we going to get up?" Nicole spun to face him. She'd been quiet while they'd trekked deeper into the woods. Maybe because the woods themselves were so quiet. Their tree house loomed ahead of them in the huge oak tree.

"The same way we did as kids?" he said.

She contemplated the tree. "I'm not sure I can climb a tree these days. I think I was a lot more spindly back then. Don't get me wrong. I exercise, but climbing trees hasn't been a specialty. The trees out in California weren't good for climbing."

"I can give you a boost." He closed the distance between them and pointed out the spot that would be easiest to climb. For the first time in a long time, his shoulders felt lighter, and his chest didn't feel as tight. The responsibility of the farm seemed far away. "Remember this was your idea."

"I haven't exactly been known for my smart decisions lately." She set the beer on the ground and positioned herself in front of the climbing route they'd zipped up as kids. "I'm counting on you not to let me land on my backside here."

She glanced at him over her shoulder. The darkness obscured the color of her eyes, but the moonlight streaming through the tree leaves gave her a glow that made her look ethereal, unworldly. He'd never noticed before she left whether she was cute or pretty; they'd always just been buds. She used to punch him in the arm for flinching. They'd had belching competitions. There'd been nothing girlie about her then.

As she hoisted herself up, he grabbed hold of her waist to help support her. From her curves to her seductive scent, she was all woman now. A very attractive woman. When she moved beyond his reach, he let go of her waist and watched her.

Her foot slipped, and his hands automatically braced her nearest body part, which happened to be her bottom.

"Thanks." Her voice was higher pitched than normal.

She lifted herself up onto the platform and then brushed her hands over her bottom. "Hand me up the beer."

He passed her the beer and studied the tree. One wrong move could pull at his chest muscles, which still bothered him from time to time. The small incision wound was healed, but the muscles still weren't quite up to full power yet.

"Are you coming, cow lifter?" Her tone was teasing. "Don't worry, I'll give you a hand if you need it. But please don't need it, because most likely we'll both fall out of the tree and break something. They won't find us for a few days. We'll have to eat grass and the fallen leaves. It might be a great diet, but we'd soil ourselves and when they found us, there'd be all sorts of questions. Why did you think climbing a tree at ten at night would be a good—"

"Would you be quiet for a moment?"

"Why? Are you afraid I'll be right?"

She was just a shadow in the tree, but he glared up at her anyway. He climbed carefully, feeling stupid the whole time. What thirty-one-year-old climbed trees besides Nicole? He'd been responsible for the farm and his brothers since he was eighteen. Even as he chastised himself for doing something so foolish, after staying inside the lines for so long, it felt good to do something just because he wanted to and not because it needed to be done.

When he reached the platform, he pulled himself up the rest of the way with only a slight protest from his chest muscles. When he straightened, she held out a beer to him.

"I knew you'd make it," she said and lowered herself to the planks of wood. She patted the spot next to her.

"There was more space up here when we were kids." When they were fourteen, they hadn't needed much space. Now there was just enough room for them to sit side by side with their shoulders touching.

At one point they'd known each other's secrets and fears, but now they were little more than strangers. All he knew about her life now was what she'd told him. It was more of an outline than the complete picture. How much would she expect him to share? How much was he willing to share?

"Did you find a new best friend after I left?" Nicole took a drink of her beer and stared up into the canopy of leaves. The stars twinkled beyond the leaves. The moon didn't overpower the stars, the way streetlights did.

"No." There was no secret in that, just a fact. "I had a group of friends in high school but never got close to any of them." Not as he'd been close to her. Because he lived out on the farm, it made it hard to connect with his friends, and with his chores, he didn't always have time.

"Do you still see any of them?" Her voice was soft in the darkness, not quite a whisper, as if they were sharing secrets and not just talking about what happened between then and now.

"Every once in a while, someone comes to town to visit their folks or something." The truth was, everyone moved away after graduation. It was rare to find anyone in Tawnee Valley between the ages of twenty and thirty who wasn't married with kids.

"I tried my hardest to fit in at my new school," Nicole said. "Mom insisted I start dressing like a girl since I wasn't living on a farm anymore. I made a few friends, but I couldn't tell them any secrets without someone spreading it around school. I certainly couldn't make blood pacts or belch in front of them." Nicole bumped his shoulder with hers.

"You were the one who wanted to do the blood thing." He took a swig of beer. It had been a while since he'd drunk alcohol, probably since Brady's wedding.

"Only because I saw it in a movie." They sat quietly for a moment. "Do you think we would have stayed friends if I hadn't moved?"

Sam took a deep breath and followed a shooting star across the sky. "Honestly? I don't know. It wasn't too long after you left that I started looking at girls differently."

"Like they grew horns and tails?"

He smiled slightly. "You know what I mean."

"Of course, but it's much more fun to tease you." She leaned her head on his shoulder. "Who knows what might have happened between us if I'd stayed?"

Would he have noticed her? As more than his friend? Would it have felt as awkward as it did now, or would they have fallen into it naturally?

She took his hand in hers and held it. "I wish I knew what to do now. I wish my future was laid out before me like yours always was."

"Don't wish that," he said harshly. No one wished for his life. Not even him.

"You have the farm. I'm sure you'll find someone who will make you an excellent farm wife, and you'll have a passel of children to help raise your livestock." She sighed. "I have an accounting degree but barely any work experience in forensic accounting. Finding another job is going to be confined to large cities. Once I start working, I won't have the time to date. I'll probably die alone, but independently wealthy because I didn't have any time to spend any of my money. Maybe I'll leave all my money to my cat. If I had a cat…"

"At least you have options." He couldn't give up his birthright, and unless he wanted to date the few eighteen-year-olds in town, he didn't have options on the dating front. There was no way he could relate to someone over a decade younger than him with her future burning bright before her, confine her to the land that had been in his family for generations. His parents had trusted him to keep the tradition going. He couldn't let them down, so he was bound to the land and cursed to be alone.

"Ugh, when did this become so serious?" She snuggled closer to him and pointed up through the branches. "What constellation is that?"

"What makes you think I know?" He tensed with her touch, but it felt nice to have someone trust him and not want to rehash the bad stuff. Someone he hadn't let down. He relaxed and drank some beer, breathing in the cool night air.

"Please." She snorted derisively. "You know everything."

He didn't know anything. All he could do was follow the path his parents laid out for him. Whether he wanted to or not. But right now, he could forget about his responsibilities for an hour and point out the stars to someone who could be his friend before she left him again.

Chapter Three

Nicole swiped at her brow with a rag. The past few days had been beyond hot. She would have loved to go hide in the air-conditioned rooms of the house, but her family was all outside working. This afternoon they planned to go over and help Sam with his fields. She figured if she tagged along with them then and didn't put in any work now, her brothers would tease her or leave her behind.

Since she left Tawnee Valley, she'd been set on a course clearly laid out before her. Get good grades to get into a good school. Meet a nice guy so she could settle down and have kids. Find a good job that would provide for the life she wanted. Live happily ever after. She'd followed the plan, and it'd backfired in her face.

Now she was back in Tawnee Valley with the guy she'd thought of so often since she'd moved away. She'd

enjoyed talking with Sam. He didn't have any expecta-
tions of her. With the exception of her little attraction
to him, he was the perfect friend. He barely talked, but
she'd always been told she talked enough for at least
two people. She didn't feel as if she needed to censor
herself around him. To be honest, though, she didn't
know what she wanted from Sam.

Friendship, definitely. He'd been her rock, even
though he hadn't actually been there. In her mind, he'd
become her diary, her confessional in the letters she'd
never sent him.

She yanked a weed out of the ground and tossed it
into the middle of the row.

More than friendship? That was the question. She really wasn't in a good place, but she couldn't sink much
lower. She was at a crossroads in life. Jeremy dump-
ing her hadn't been as painful as it should have been.
She'd spent seven years waiting for him. It was almost
a relief when he broke it off. At least she finally knew
how he felt.

Losing her job had hurt more. She'd never been let
go before. She'd done a good job, shown up to work on
time. Never questioned her boss or the extra work. Always tried to be a team player. How was she supposed
to know that the company would downsize?

When she found a new job, wherever it ended up
being, she would move there. It wasn't as if Tawnee
Valley or the surrounding community had a job opening for a forensic accountant. The big-city accounting
firms and possibly the FBI were her best bets. In the
past couple of days, she'd started her search and sent
out résumés to every posting she could find.

After being cooped up and staring at the screen all day, being outside, even in the blistering heat, felt great.

"Nikki's slacking again, Dad," Ethan shouted.

She spun around to give Ethan a dirty look. "I can't believe you are tattling on me. You're twenty-five years old."

"Maybe if you'd get your butt in gear, I wouldn't have to tell on you." Ethan winked before he disappeared down one of the lines of corn.

"You don't have to be out here, Nik." Her father walked over and stood beside her.

"Please call me Nicole." The old nicknames shouldn't bother her, but she hadn't been called any of them for the past couple of decades. They just sounded weird. Besides, why wouldn't she want to be out here? "I like helping out."

Her dad looked down the rows of corn. It was as tall as they were and would be harvested in the next few weeks. "It's a lot of hard work, but at least it's honest work."

She put her arm around his waist and leaned against his side for only a second. After all, they were hot and sweaty, but that didn't mean a side hug wasn't nice. "You're a good man, Dad."

"Wish your mom had thought so." He took his hat off and hit it across his thigh. "Sun's a bear today."

That was about as emotional as her father got, whereas her mother was emotional all the time. "Yup, it's pretty hot out."

"Make sure to get that weed over there and check for bugs." Her father disappeared behind another row.

They'd been out all morning, since 6:00 a.m. She was looking forward to a nice, long shower before running into Sam. Not that she was going to get pretty just to muck about in the muddy pen to drive the hogs into the trailer. But she could at least get rid of a layer of sweat before he saw her.

Maybe she'd sneak away now to get that shower. She glanced around to see if her father or brothers were nearby. Smiling, she spun toward the house and slammed straight into someone.

Strong hands grabbed her shoulders, and when she drew in a breath filled with a manly scent, she knew immediately whose chest she'd almost broken her nose on.

She grinned up at him while rubbing her nose. "Hey, Sam. What are you doing in our field?"

"Working." He set her back slightly.

She must be disgusting. Even her hair felt sticky. She didn't even bother to run a hand through her hair or try to primp at all. It couldn't be helped.

"I thought I wouldn't see you until we came over to help with the hogs." She rubbed her gloved hands over her backside, trying to brush off some of the dirt that had surely accumulated there when she'd pulled the last dozen or so weeds. "So what are you doing over here? Did they tell you I wasn't pulling my weight? Because I can pull a mean weed. Wait, I know! It's because I don't know all the bug names, isn't it?"

"If I help over here, it'll go quicker." Sam shifted his weight from one foot to the other. He had on jeans and a long-sleeved shirt as she did. While it kept the plants from cutting up her arms, it didn't help with the heat. However, he looked as if he'd just stepped out of the shower. His dark hair was slicked back under a cap. The sun made his blue eyes seem even deeper as it drew out the darker shades. She pulled her gaze from those eyes before she lost herself in them or said something stupid.

"That's great," she said. "Maybe you can tell me what some of these bugs are called. I think Dad and the brats avoid me because they know I'll talk their ear off if they come near. But you don't mind if I talk, do you?" She watched his face carefully.

He shrugged but looked distinctly uncomfortable, as if he really would like her to just remain quiet but didn't want to upset her. If he wasn't going to protest, she'd talk his ear off because she liked chatting with him. Even if he was just being polite, she couldn't help her smile.

"I knew I could count on you."

When she moved to grab her bucket, he held up a hand. "No hugs."

She laughed. "Oh, trust me, I'm not hugging anyone smelling like I do. I don't believe in sharing sweat when hugging. Don't worry, though…I'll just hug you more next time."

When he grimaced, she laughed again.

"You'll get used to it. I swear." She bent down to pull another weed.

He walked beside her silently, pulling weeds as he went. Investigating the leaves and corncobs. Occasionally he'd point out an insect and let her know whether it was beneficial or needed to be gotten rid of.

She talked about nonsense the entire time. He didn't respond, but it didn't bother her. She was glad for the company. She got only that partial smile, though. Not even a flash of dimple. What would it take to make Sam Ward smile? When her mind started turning over certain ways to make a man like Sam smile, she bent down to tie her shoe to hide her suddenly red face. When they made it to the end of her row, her father was there.

"John," Sam acknowledged.

"You ready for us?" Dad put his hand in his pocket and pulled out a handkerchief to wipe the sweat from his brow.

"The trailer is at the gate, ready for loading."

"Good, good." Her father turned to her as if noticing her for the first time. "You coming with, kid?"

She hated it when he called her "kid." Even "Nik" was better than "kid." "Yeah. I was hoping to take a quick shower first, though."

"No need," her father said. "Just going to get muddy anyway. Come on."

They followed him down the hill, where Ethan and Wes waited next to their dad's truck.

"Why don't you ride with Sam?" Dad said and left them to join the boys.

"Well, that's not at all awkward." Nicole smiled up at Sam. "Do you have room for me?"

He nodded and led the way over to his truck. He pulled open the passenger door, and she climbed into the truck.

She slid off her gloves and put them in her lap, suddenly very conscious of the small space and her current lack of personal hygiene. Her deodorant had given up at least a half hour ago, and while she would have loved to believe her sweat didn't stink…she was fairly certain she didn't smell like a bed of roses right now, but more like the fertilizer. "Sorry for the smell. Normally I bathe before getting into enclosed spaces with other people."

"It doesn't bother me." He started the truck and drove up the driveway.

"I suppose when you work with cows, pigs and sheep all day, one stinky human isn't overwhelming." She turned to watch his expression.

"You don't stink." His tone didn't imply anything negative or even positive, but the simple comment made her heart sing a little.

"Thanks, but you don't have to be nice. After all, I'm about to climb into your hog pen and get all muddy. I'm sure the hogs won't mind the smell." She glanced out the window as they passed the field where their tree house was. Friends didn't care if other friends liked the way they smelled. She didn't know how to act around him. So she did what she did best—talk. "I don't think I've carried my cell phone around with me at all. It's odd because I always checked it in LA. But the reception is so iffy at Dad's that I just don't bother. The funny thing is, I don't really feel like I'm missing anything."

"Don't you have friends who call?" Sam asked.

"Funny thing, that." She twisted in her seat to face him. "Jeremy got our friends. Turns out they were mostly his to start. The friends I had in college all went their separate ways, but we email once in a while."

The lack of people to hang out with had made her decision to head back to her dad's that much easier. She could just imagine what Jeremy was saying about her now that she was gone. For all she knew, he'd already hooked up with someone new. She could name at least two girls in their group of friends who had always wanted him. That gave her pause. Nicole must still be in the numb phase of the breakup, because that didn't hurt as much as it would have a few months ago. Or would it have hurt then?

Sam turned down his driveway and pulled up next to the barn. She snapped out of her thoughts.

"How many hogs are we loading?" She wished she could find a way to make him talk for longer than a minute and finally see his smile. If he was gorgeous sullen, would he be stunningly handsome full-on smiling?

"A dozen." He opened his door and got out. Before he could reach her side, she opened her door and hopped down in front of him.

"A baker's or literal?" Maybe if she were funnier, he would smile. She never was good at jokes or funny stories. Her jokes tended to meander too much, and she always screwed up the punch line.

"Literal." Not even a crack of a smile. Though she swore she saw a little merriment in his eyes.

"Awesome." She followed him down to the pen. Her father and brothers joined them.

"Spread out around the outside and then we'll slowly work them forward," Sam said and handed her a square board about three feet by three feet and less than an inch thick. It had cutouts for her hands. "If they get past you, don't worry, but try to keep them in the circle we create."

He could read the directions to build an IKEA chair and his deep voice would hold her enthralled. Maybe that was the way to get him to talk: read instructions. He raised his eyebrow at her when she didn't respond. She nodded.

"Don't slip up." Wes winked as he passed her.

She wished she'd never taught those two brats to wink. The way they did it was obnoxious, as if they knew exactly what she was thinking about. Ideally Sam didn't. He didn't need to know that she had the equivalent of a schoolgirl crush on him. It wasn't as if she was drawing hearts with their initials in her notebook or anything like that. All he needed to know was that she wanted them to be friends again.

They all moved into the pen, and Sam showed her where to stand before going to his place near the gate. The poor pigs sensed something was up and moved away from them.

When Sam nodded, they all started working the hogs. Moving them out of their comfortable home and into a trailer seemed cruel, but she wasn't about to become a vegetarian over it. She liked her bacon too much to give it up.

The majority of the hogs were blocked in, and her brothers helped Sam get them into the smaller run that would lead them to the trailer. Of course, the ornery one had to be near her. She pushed it with the tip of the board, but it merely rolled on its side in the mud. The chaos in the rest of the pen hadn't reached this one's brain yet. Or it just didn't care. Maybe it didn't have a brain. One too many dunks in the mud pit, perhaps.

"You're making me look bad," she muttered to the pig. It snorted in response. Maybe a different tactic was in order. "What if I promised you some good slop tonight? The very best carrots and potatoes? What if I dump my whole plate in your slop bin? You'd like that, wouldn't you?"

The pig finally got up and meandered toward the gate.

"Good pig. Who's going to get a big apple with dinner tonight?" She followed behind with her board positioned between the pig and her. "The biggest pig in here, that's who."

Proud of herself and her pig, she couldn't help beaming at Sam as the animal kept heading his way. His gaze followed the hog, but then those blue eyes focused on her and she stopped in her tracks. His lips curved into a smile so genuine that her grip loosened on the board and her heart beat a little harder.

As if sensing her resolve slipping away, the pig turned. It happened so quickly she didn't have time to brace herself before the hog plowed into the side of her board and around her. She tried to turn, but the ground beneath her feet was wet for the pigs to wallow in, and the ground slipped out from under her. She set the board into the mud to try to keep herself from falling.

Ethan and Wes would never let her live it down if she fell into the pig muck.

Sam couldn't do anything but watch as Nicole's feet went out from beneath her. The twins were already after the last hog. Sam rushed over to where she fell and knelt in the muck next to her. His pulse raced with fear. She could be hurt. The mud squished beneath the knees of his jeans. The wetness reached his skin. The board lay across her chest. She'd landed faceup in pigpen mud. It covered her back from head to toe.

"If he thinks he's getting an apple now," she muttered angrily, "he has another think coming. I can't wait to have bacon when I get up. And maybe some ham."

Sam couldn't help the smile that touched his lips or the relief that flooded through him when he realized she was okay. Even down, she kept talking. He pulled the board off her and tossed it to the side. When he turned back to Nicole, she looked at him as if he were an alien.

"What?"

"Oh, don't stop. Darn it. I finally get a full smile and it's over before I can fully appreciate it." She pushed up on her elbows. The mud sucked at her back and hair. Her face scrunched up. "Oh, that's so gross."

"I smile." He pulled off his brown work glove and brushed some mud off her cheek with his thumb. The touch hadn't been anything other than an attempt to clean off her cheek before the dirt got in her mouth, but electricity sizzled through his blood. He almost missed her slight intake of breath and widened eyes, as if she felt it, too.

"I'm not sure I can get out of this…mud." Her smile was softer than the normal grins she gave him. "Would you mind giving me a lift, please?"

He nodded and stood, leaning over and offering his hand. She grabbed his wrist, and he yanked her up. He hadn't been thinking. The motion pulled something in his chest near his scar. It was enough to take his breath away for a moment.

"Sam? Are you okay?" Her bare hands touched his cheeks, and she lifted his head until she was looking into his eyes. At some point, she must have taken off her filthy gloves. Her forehead was wrinkled with concern.

He focused on the mixture of green and gold within her eyes and took slow breaths, willing the pain away. The color was soothing, like a field of spring grass, soft and damp with morning dew. Her eyes searched his, as if she was looking for some reason why he was acting as if he were an old man trying to catch his breath.

"I'm okay." He straightened away from her hands

and took in a full breath. He rubbed at his chest. He'd felt like an old man before the surgery on his heart. The doctor assured him that he'd feel young again once he was done healing.

"Did I hurt you?" She covered his hand on his chest with her own. "I'm going to blame the mud, because surely I don't weigh that much if you can bench-press a bull."

He smiled. He couldn't help it. Heck, he didn't want to help it. She always said the oddest things. "I thought it was a cow."

"If I weren't covered in more mud and…ew, other stuff than you, I would so hug you right now, Sam Ward."

"I'll remember that next time you try to hug me." He gave her a half smile, which seemed to please her to no end. He hoped she'd forgotten about his chest pain. He didn't want to see that look of concern that always filled his brothers' eyes when they looked at him. He'd had a bum valve. It was all fixed now and he should have no issues living his life. Except the odd strain on the healing scar.

"I don't suppose you are going to let me into your truck looking like this." Her eyes danced as she met his gaze.

"Brush the mud off and quit playing around, Nik."

Nicole winced at her father's voice. "I'm not playing, Dad. I'm fairly certain this is more than a brush-the-mud-off situation."

"Oh, I can't go on, either," Wes yelled. His green eyes twinkled with mischief. "I have a little mud on my pants. I can't help anymore. I think I'll go inside and play Xbox for the rest of the day."

"Shut it, Wes," her dad said. His gaze went over Sam and her. "Looks like neither of you are up to going into the sale barn, Sam. The boys and I can take the hogs in for you. Hose her down and send her home if you don't mind, Sam."

Sam watched the emotions run through Nicole's eyes. Pain, embarrassment, resignation.

"Yeah, I'll make sure she gets home. Thanks, John," Sam said.

Before the twins were born, Nicole had been John's little helper. After the boys, though, no matter how much she acted like one, her father still preferred to spend his time with them. She could never find her way back into the favorite slot. These were just a few of the secrets shared between best friends in the tree house they'd built.

He couldn't imagine the pain of having her folks split their family in half. What must that have felt like for her? Had she felt like the last one to get picked? If her mother hadn't moved so far away, would Sam and Nicole have been split up?

"You ready to get hosed down?" he asked as the truck doors slammed behind them.

She lifted her eyebrow at him. "You aren't serious."

"How else are you going to get all the pig smell off you?" Sam flicked a chunk of mud from her shoulder. "I can't exactly let you into the house looking like that."

Her smile was downright wicked when she stepped close to him. "If I'm going to get hosed down, then you are, too."

She put a handful of mud from her leg on the front of his shirt and smiled up at him. "Just so you know, if you hadn't grown so big, I'd have just tackled you in the mud."

The images she conjured in his mind were enough to make him welcome the cold hose water. The truck engine vanished into the distance, leaving him and Nicole alone. If she wanted to play with mud, he decided two could play at this game.

Chapter Four

Nicole took one look at the mischievous look in Sam's eyes and knew she was in trouble. So when he bent over to scoop up some mud, she shoved him off balance.

"Hey!" He fell to the side and into the mud. She took the opportunity to turn to make her getaway.

If the mud hadn't sucked down her boots, she might have made it, too.

As she tried to pull free of the mud, Sam said, "Not so fast, Nikki."

His hand wrapped around her calf and yanked her backward. She lost her balance and fell backward on top of him. The air rushed out of her lungs, but at least he was more solid than the mud beneath his back.

"I hope your plan was for me to squish you more into the mud and get more on you," Nicole said. She started to struggle to get up, but his hands on her hips stopped her.

"If you squirm any more, we are going to have more than just a mud problem," he said through his teeth.

Heat rushed to her cheeks. She glanced over her shoulder. Sam half leaned out of the mud, but he was definitely more covered in it than she was. A spark of heat in his eyes made her aware of the intimacy of their position. The warmth of him against her backside surged through her. If it hadn't stunk like crazy and the flies weren't trying to bite every piece of mud from her body, she might have been tempted to…

She looked away. He was probably worried about an elbow to his crotch, and here she was getting all hot and bothered while covered in mud and…stuff. She took a deep breath and instantly regretted it. It was the other stuff that made her wrinkle her nose.

Needing to keep things easy, she glanced back again and flashed him a grin. "Afraid I'll get more mud on you?"

"I don't think that's possible." He pushed her up by her hips until she could regain her footing. "And here I thought you'd play fair."

She turned to watch him peel himself out of the mud. "There's nothing fair about your height or weight advantage. You just fall easy."

He raised his eyebrow at her as he stood up. "Maybe unbalanced in a pigpen, I fall easy."

She shook off what mud she could. This wasn't exactly facial or soothing mud bath material. "It's starting to itch."

"That's because it's drying. We should go over to the hose." He started to lead the way out of the pen.

"You aren't serious about the hose?" When he didn't

respond, she added, "Seriously? When there is a perfectly good hot shower in the house?"

He stopped and faced her. "We're not allowed to track mud through the house."

"Isn't it *your* house?" She crossed her arms. "If I'd known about the lack of warm water facilities, I would have fallen in the mud at my own house."

"You're welcome to walk home." He gestured for her to go ahead.

There was a lot of land between the two houses, and going the road way wouldn't be any better. Screw that. "Oh, no. You drove me here, and you'll be driving me back."

"I suppose you could ride in the truck bed, but only after I've had a chance to shower and change."

She weighed her options. Cold and dripping wet followed by a nice warm shower or being eaten alive by flies and itching from the drying mud for some unknown amount of time? She could feel Sam watching her as she made her decision. "What will I change into?"

His eyes flared hot for a second before his cool demeanor slipped back into place. Probably just her imagination running wild. To Sam she'd always just been that annoying tomboy from next door, who happened to be his best friend.

"I'm sure I can find you a T-shirt and sweats," he said.

"Somehow I don't think we are the same size like we were way back when," she grumbled. She'd always liked wearing her boyfriend's shirts, but she needed to remember Sam was just a friend, even if wearing his clothes seemed intimate. "I suppose I'll let you hose me down, but on one condition." She held up her finger.

"What's that?" The corner of his mouth twitched.

She narrowed her eyes and shook her finger at him. "As long as you don't like it."

A laugh burst from his lips. Her heart skipped a beat at the sound as she smiled up at him. It didn't last long, but it soothed her to know that he still could laugh.

His mouth settled into a small smile that made her catch her breath. "I'll try. But you better not have any fun hosing me down, either. This isn't the water balloon fight of '95."

Shaking off the sudden feelings of giddiness bubbling under the surface, she said, "Okay, hug on it."

He held out his hands. "No—"

As if that would stop her. She stepped into his arms and squeezed him around the waist. The mud on them made weird smacking noises. She laughed as she released him. "See, that wasn't so bad."

"Says you." He continued toward the back of the house where the hose was. Hose water was hose water, and she'd never had a warm soak from a hose. The water out here was either from the well or the cistern. Either way, it would be frigid underground water, regardless of the warm weather.

"Don't you have a pond that we can jump into?" She stopped a few feet away from him as he went to turn the hose on.

"Not unless you want to get eaten by mosquitoes." He turned the handle, and the rush of water could be heard flooding through the line. He picked up the other end of the hose as the water cascaded to the ground. "Besides, it's a runoff from the hog pens. You'd get cleaner from rolling in the pens."

The spray created a rainbow. Of course, a rainbow

would normally be a happy thing, but not when it was created by water from the Arctic.

"Wait." She held up her hands to ward off the oncoming blast of cold water. "What if I just take off my clothes?"

"I don't think—"

His words stopped the second she started unbuttoning her shirt. "It's not like we'd be naked. I have on a bra and underwear, and I'm sure you are wearing some sort of underwear. The mud would mostly be our heads, which would be just fine walking through your house. Not that our heads walk, but—"

"Nicole." Her name was gruff, almost strangled, on his lips.

"I'm just trying to make it easier on us." She stopped unbuttoning her shirt and glanced up at him, uncertain of what she was going to see.

His eyes were glued to her hands as they hovered over the last button. She watched in fascination as he swallowed. Her skin prickled, and it had nothing to do with the heat or the drying mud. She had thought to avoid the chill of the hose water, but at the intensity of his gaze, she would almost have welcomed the cold.

Try as she might, she couldn't deny the attraction in his eyes or the desire burning beneath her skin. Even covered in…stuff. Oh, she was in trouble. And she didn't know how deep she wanted to dig herself. She could laugh this off and pretend she didn't see or feel what was happening between them. Deny this intense longing to just go with her gut for the first time in a long time.

Her gut was saying go for it. What was the worst that could happen? It wasn't as if she'd fall for the boy next door. What was sex between old friends? Would he be up for a roll in the hay with no obligations? Or was he looking for more at this point in his life?

It didn't matter. If Sam had wanted to act on this attraction, he would have. The men she'd been with had always taken the initiative. If a man wanted to kiss you, he'd kiss you. Right? She needed to get it through her head that this wasn't happening between them. They were just friends. Not even real friends. Friends from childhood.

"I think this is the quietest I've been in a long time." She tried to laugh, but it came out stilted.

He lifted his gaze to hers, and she took an involuntary step back. The intensity of his eyes struck some primal need deep inside her. Whoa, who would have known that Sam Ward was the type of guy who could melt her into a puddle with just a look? If she felt this way from a look, what would happen if he actually touched her? Goose bumps rose on her exposed skin. That was a very dangerous idea. As much as she longed to finish taking off her shirt and let whatever happens happen, she wasn't sure she could handle the intensity of Sam. Maybe being partially naked in front of him wasn't a great idea, even if the alternative was freezing cold water.

She pulled her shirt together. The mud squished between her fingers.

"You know, the hose probably won't be that bad." Lord knew her flesh needed cooling down. She flinched but braced herself for the cold. "Go ahead. Spray me."

Eighty-five. Eighty-six. Eighty-seven. If Sam kept counting, he could fight this urge to walk over and finish stripping Nicole naked. He started counting the second he caught sight of Nicole's hot-pink bra under the dull flannel shirt. Its little bow seemed to beckon him with its innocent temptation. It'd been almost easy to think of her as one of the guys with her body completely covered. Almost. It had been a hell of a lot easier before seeing that flash of femininity.

As he'd counted in his head, she'd innocently revealed a bit more of her skin. She hadn't even been aware of what she was doing to him. The low simmer of desire that pulsed through his veins every time she was close was now a full boil. He was barely managing to keep it from boiling over.

"Are you going to do it?" She squeezed her eyes shut, bracing herself. She'd covered herself, but the image was burned into his retinas. Satin pale skin that looked soft yet stretched over muscles that were clearly toned. His fingertips twitched with the need to feel if it really was as soft and lush as it looked.

Ninety-four. He looked up into the sky. Maybe a plane would fall on him. Just a few more numbers and surely he'd be able to focus again. Ninety-five.

Her voice had that what-are-you-doing tone to it when she said, "Sam."

He sighed. Was it possible for Nicole to stay quiet for longer than a minute? At least give him long enough to calm the throbbing inside. Ninety-six.

"Am I going to have to hose myself down?"

When he looked at her, she had exactly the stance he imagined she'd have. One hand on her hip and one hand holding her shirt together. The only thing missing was a tapping foot. She still looked tempting as hell.

This was ridiculous. He took a deep breath and raced

through the numbers until he reached a hundred. A grown man should be able to be near an attractive woman without thinking of her in a sexual way. Obviously he needed to work on growing up more. He held the hose out to her, not trusting himself to keep from making a fool out of himself. Besides, the cold water would do him good. "Maybe you should hose me down first."

She buttoned her middle button, leaving way too much skin showing for his comfort, and then grabbed the hose from him. The water formed a muddy area in the grass. She screwed up her face, and he knew she was going to argue with him. Nothing was ever easy with Nicole. "Are you sure about this? I could turn around, and you could take off your clothes, and then I can—"

"Just do it, Nicole." He bit out the words from between his clenched teeth.

She held the hose up and smiled a little too gleefully. "If you insist."

She pressed her thumb over the spout and created a spray. The water was cool as it hit his chest and soaked through his shirt. It didn't do much to cool the burning desire within him, but it was better than nothing.

"Turn around and I'll get your back," Nicole said loudly over the sound of splattering mud and water.

He turned, and the ice-cold water soaked the back of his shirt and denims. As the water started to weigh down his jeans, he realized he hadn't thought this through. His jeans would be near impossible to get off wet, but it wasn't as if he could throw them in the wash covered in mud. And he wasn't about to take them off here with Nicole watching. She'd realize how much she affected him. Cold water or not.

"Take off your shirt."

"What?" He turned and got a face full of water.

"Oops." Laughing, she lowered the hose and held up her hands. "I swear I didn't mean to do that."

Her smile had that little hint of mischief in it. He wasn't sure if she'd meant to spray him in the face or not.

"I'm not sure I believe that," he mumbled as he swiped the water from his face. He wasn't in any condition to get retribution without acting on the latent desire burning in his veins.

"Take off your shirt and I'll get your head." She tossed the hose between her hands like a gunslinger and kept that grin on her face.

"You already got me in the face." He started unbuttoning his shirt. "Not sure what you need me to take off my soggy, dirty shirt for. It's not like it could get much dirtier."

"Your hair is filled with dried mud. It'd be a lot easier to get the back of it without your collar in the way." That was way too reasonable for Nicole.

He narrowed his eyes at her. She was up to something. He just didn't know what yet. Even though the water was cold, the air was still hot. Getting out of his shirt seemed like a good plan to cool down his body from the heat of the day and the heat of his desire for Nicole.

He turned his back to her as he shrugged out of his shirt and tossed it over to the porch. "Hit me."

A second passed and then another, but no blast of cold hit him. Just when he was going to turn around to ask her about it, she cleared her throat.

"Sure." Her voice was a little higher in pitch, but before he could turn around to figure out what she was thinking, a blast of cold water hit the back of his head.

Mud started to streak down his face. "Hold up!"

The water retreated. "What?"

He looked over his shoulder at her and raised his eyebrow, dislodging some mud in the process so that it ran down his cheek.

"What, you can't handle a little mud in your eyes?"

"No, and I don't care for it in my mouth, either."

Giggling, she glanced around the yard.

"Okay, new plan." Nicole walked toward him. She pointed over to a stump from the tree he had cut down last year. "Sit down. You really are too tall, you know. You should have stopped growing at least a foot ago. It would make you so much easier to deal with."

"You mean you could get your way easier?" He wasn't sure where that had come from. He wasn't normally someone who teased people. But Nicole wasn't some people. She talked whenever he stopped and ordered him around as if she had some right to. When they'd been kids, she'd always been the boss. Whether she was the king—because queen was too feminine for the tomboy Nicole had been—or the head cowboy, Nicole had been determined to have her way. Back then, he'd been more than happy to let her lead him around. Now…he wasn't so sure.

He kept his back to her but glanced her way.

"Exactly. If you didn't practice lifting cows every day and grow to an impractical height, it would be a lot easier to make you do my bidding." She closed the distance between them and squinted up at him. "If I'd known you were going to get so tall, I would have kept growing."

He smiled over his shoulder at her. "Like you had a choice in the matter."

She gave him her best serious expression, which was a feat given the amount of mud on her head and face. "Of course I had a choice. Now go sit down so I can rinse the mud out of your hair. Then you can do the same for me."

He shook his head but went over to the stump and sat down. The cold water had barely taken the edge off his desire. A desire he shouldn't even have. Even if she weren't here temporarily, Nicole deserved better than someone like him. He destroyed every relationship he touched. Both his brothers hadn't talked to him for years after he'd messed up their lives. It wasn't until recently that he'd tried to make things right with them. But it still niggled at the back of his brain that he would screw it up for them again and destroy the happiness they'd finally found. They were better off without him in their lives. Nicole would be better off when she left, too.

That thought affected the burning in his veins, leaving him slightly chilled on the inside.

"Okay, hmm…" Nicole still stood behind him. He could hear the water splashing on the roots of the tree.

"What's wrong?" He didn't bother turning around. What did it matter what he felt or didn't feel? He was no good to anyone. "Just get it done."

"Okay, Mr. Grumpy Pants," she muttered. "Lean your head back so the mud doesn't get in your eyes."

He closed his eyes and did as she asked. Her fingers brushed his hair over his ear as the cold water flooded his scalp. She ran her hands through his hair, and something hot and needy jolted inside him.

His hand closed around her wrist to stop the motion of her hand. "What are you doing?"

"Picking flowers," she said in a flat tone. "Gee, Sam, I'm just getting the mud out of your hair, not trying to suck your brains out or anything."

He was an ass. Nicole was just trying to be nice and take care of him. She was being the friend that he used to have. And all he could think about was the fact that she was so close to him that he could lean back and feel the heat of her skin against his back. That he could turn and have her in his arms and feel the softness of her lips pressed against his. What kind of friend was he that whenever she was near him, all he could think about was kissing her?

"Are you going to let go of my hand so I can finish?"

"What? Yeah." He released her wrist. The sooner she finished, the sooner he could get away from her.

Her fingers stroking his scalp were torture. It had been a long time since he'd had anyone touch him that way. It wasn't sexual, but it wasn't casual, either. Relaxing, comforting, but with that zing of attraction.

"I always wondered about you." Her words were barely audible above the flow of water.

"Wondered?" He dared not to open his eyes and look up into her face. A man had only so much resistance, and his was sorely tried. Even with all his doubts, the only things that welled within him were the facts that she was Nicole and he burned for her. He hadn't even hosed her down yet. Maybe he could do that with his eyes closed.

Her fingers slid over his ear and through his hair. "You know, things like what you were doing. If you had a girlfriend. If you were happy."

He grunted. They'd covered all that the other night. The water didn't seem so cold with her touching him.

"I never wondered about your job, though. It seems like you were always destined for this farm, and it was always yours." She brushed his hair with her free hand, and he almost wished she had both hands free to work through his hair. "Though I could see you as a fire-fighter or cop."

"Not a doctor like Luke or whatever it is that Brady does at that company he works for?" Next to his brothers, he was nothing. He never even went to college because Dad died and Mom got sick. He had been needed here on the farm, and he'd been happy to do what he could for his family. "What did Jeremy do?"

"Jeremy?" She sounded as if she didn't know who Jeremy was. That made Sam smile. Maybe he affected her, too. "Oh, Jeremy. He was an investment banker. Totally boring job."

But Sam bet it paid good money. Not like the farm, which barely earned enough to keep food on his table. He'd had a few good years and worked some temporary jobs in the winter to keep up with the bills, but he'd barely been afloat when Brady had come back to town. Sam was not exactly the type of man who attracted women. At least not the type of woman who would stay and be part of his life.

"When he would talk about his job, my eyes would feel heavy, and I swear I would nap a little while listening to him." Nicole brushed her hand through the water over his bare shoulder. "He never did listen to me, anyway."

The muscles in his shoulder twitched at her touch. Even if he could have gotten words past his thickened throat, Sam didn't know what to say to that. How could someone not listen to her? She talked all the time, but her voice had a soothing quality about it that made it almost musical instead of annoying.

Instead of saying anything, he took a deep breath. His breath was shaky from her touch.

"All clean," she announced, and he felt the loss of her warmth when she stepped back. "That didn't seem so bad. Here you go. Do your worst."

He turned and reached for the hose in her outstretched hand. Her smile froze on her face as she stared at his chest. He'd almost forgotten.

She reached out and touched the healing scar from his surgery. "What happened?"

He hissed, but not from pain. Heat raced through him. Her touch was like burning coals on his body.

"Does it hurt?" She stared up at him with her huge green eyes. "Sam? This is a fresh scar. What is it from? Did you hurt yourself? No wonder you were in pain lifting me from the ground. Why didn't you tell me? I would have managed to get up on my own, though you were definitely helpful, but I wouldn't want to hurt you."

"I had surgery."

She stared at the scar, trying to piece together what had needed operation. The scar was on his left pectoral muscle. She could probably feel the rapid beat of his heart beneath her palm. Her hands shook, and when she lifted her eyes to look at him, tears swam in them. "Your heart?"

He nodded.

"But…" A tear slipped over the edge and left a clean track in the dried mud along her cheek. "But…"

Nicole's upset was something he wasn't used to.

Brady had been matter-of-fact about it, and Luke had been angry, but neither of them had cried about it. Even Sam hadn't cried about it. It was what it was, and now it was over. "It's okay, Nicole."

"No, it's not." She shook her head and pressed her palm over his heart as if she could heal it through her touch alone. "Why didn't you tell me? When did this happen? Are you going to die? Is your heart fixed? I've gone on and on about me and my problems, but oh, my God, Sam…"

She pressed her trembling lips together as if she was trying to hold back a sob.

"I'm not dying." Sam hadn't really spoken about his heart to anyone outside of his immediate family, though most of Tawnee Valley knew. That was the way it was with a small community. "I had a valve that needed to be replaced. No big deal."

"Are you just trying to make me feel better, or are you telling me the truth? Because, so help me God, Sam Ward, if you die on me, I will never forgive you." Her relieved smile didn't quite make it to her eyes.

"I'm not ready to die yet." Sam covered her hand with his. He meant it, too. He'd hardly lived. His life had been this farm and taking care of his brothers. And now he didn't know what he wanted, but he wanted more. More than this farm and the solitude it forced on him. More than living a life that was forced on him because his parents died too early.

"Good. Now be a good guy and hose me down before the flies eat me alive." She slid her hand out from under his and stepped back. "I'm warning you, though—scar or no scar—if you don't play fair, I will wrestle that hose away from you and make you pay."

His chest felt lighter at her grin. Whenever Luke or Brady looked at him, even now, there was always this glint of concern or worry in their eyes, but not Nicole. She accepted the fact that he said he was fine, and she acted as if nothing had happened.

"Sure." He lifted the hose and sprayed.

"Oh, my God, that is cold." She danced around but stayed in the stream. "I don't know how you stood there silently while I hosed you off. If I'd known you were just taking it like a man, I would have said never mind, I'll let the flies eat me alive. I even thought it'd feel good in this heat, but I was wrong. It feels damned cold. Cold, cold, cold."

He couldn't help his smile.

She spun and he continued to hose down her back, but when she started to shrug out of her shirt, he lowered the spray.

"What are you doing?" he got out around the frog in his throat.

She glanced over her shoulder with a mischievous look. "Why, I'm just making sure you'll be able to do as good a job as I did."

Before he could protest further, she chucked her shirt over to where he'd left his. Only her pink bra interrupted the silky skin of her back.

As she sat on the tree stump, she reached up and pulled out the band holding her dark hair in a ponytail. "Ew, please don't judge me on the cleanliness of my hair, because normally I don't go rolling around in pigpens."

He swallowed. He could do this. It was no different than seeing her in a bathing suit. They'd seen each other in bathing suits growing up, but Nicole hadn't developed back then. She was all woman now. From her narrow waist to her curved hips. He didn't dare look at her front. He already knew from their multiple hugs that she'd developed quite nicely up top.

"I'm ready when you are." She tipped her head back, looking up at the sky, and leaned back, pressing her hands against the stump.

He glanced at his dirty, waterlogged shirt and almost went over to put it on. Maybe the drape of his shirt would hide the fact that he was turned on.

"Come on, Sam." She glanced over at him. "You aren't afraid of me, are you? That I'll ravish you when you least expect it? I promise not to bite…hard."

Screw it. He walked over, and she smiled as if she'd won, tipped her head back and closed her eyes. He lifted the hose and let the water pour over her hair. He meant to keep his eyes on her hair, but the way she held her body thrust her breasts up too nicely for him not to notice. They were as perfect as he'd imagined. He wished he hadn't imagined them, but ever since Nicole came back into his life, all he could think about was her.

What was she thinking? What was she doing? What was she wearing? What did her lips taste like? What did her skin feel like? Would making love to her feel the same as when he hugged her? Warm and comfortable, like a missing piece of himself. Or hot and unpredictable, like the words that cascaded out of her mouth.

"Use your hand," she said, and he about dropped the hose.

"What?" His muscles twitched from resisting using his hands to feel her velvety skin, but that couldn't be what she meant.

"In my hair," she said. "Use your hand to get out

some of the mud, or else it will all be going down your drain in the shower I plan to take after this. And if your pipes are anything like Dad's, then you don't need all that muck going down them."

Sam sighed and looked up to the sky as if to ask, "Why me?" Hadn't he been tested enough? This was just another chore. Another job. If he didn't think about it, maybe he could just get through it quickly and be done. But the minute he touched her hair with the water rushing over his fingertips, he knew he wouldn't be able to ignore the growing heat between them.

Beneath the mud, her hair was silken strands running through his fingers. He rubbed at a particularly stubborn piece of mud.

"Mmm, that feels good." The husky tone of her voice was rich with the pleasure she was feeling and made his wet jeans even tighter. She practically purred, "Don't stop, Sam."

Though Sam was a bit rusty on the dating and friendship side of things, his body definitely believed this was more than friendly. His pulse raced as if he'd had to run down the bull in the neighbor's yard. Either Nicole was unconsciously sexy as hell or she was inviting him down a road they probably shouldn't travel.

"I always loved having my hair washed." Nicole opened her eyes, and he found himself caught in her gaze. Never-ending layers of light green, complex and simple all at once. "Could you imagine what it would have been like in the days when people used to help you bathe and dress? I've actually gone to the salon just for a shampoo before. It always seems so decadent. Paying someone to do something you could do yourself. Not that I'm lazy about washing my own hair…

but you've got some amazing hands. You could make a lot of money washing hair, but I probably wouldn't want to share you. I'll keep you my own little secret for when I find myself dunked in mud."

Her eyes drifted shut, but her lips curved into a satisfied smile. She was just spouting nonsense. That was Nicole. Words just flowed out of her. Ideas layered upon unsuspecting words. He knew he should take his hand out of her hair, that the water had taken most of the mud out of her hair, but he couldn't help himself. She practically purred when he ran his fingers along her scalp and through her hair. His body was stiff from repressed desire. He caught water in his hand and ran it along her cheekbone, brushing over the dirt with his thumb until it disappeared.

"Nicole?" He pushed out her name, needing someone else to end this dangerous game, knowing he never could.

She opened her eyes. Her pupils were dilated, and her breathing had quickened. His gaze caught on the rise and fall of her breasts with every breath. Her lips parted in an invitation he wasn't strong enough to deny.

He dropped the hose as she rose to stand before him. Her chin tipped up to offer him her perfect lips. Blood raced through his veins, taking away any reasoning. Leaving him with only the burning desire to taste her lips.

She placed her hands over his racing heart but didn't push him away. "Sam."

His name was a beacon on her lips, drawing him down until only a whisper was between them. Even though he truly wanted this, he knew it was wrong. Wrong for her.

He searched her eyes, looking for the strength he needed to back away, but all he saw was an open invitation in her sweet smile, the acceptance of what was happening between them. No judgment, no pity, only desire. New beginnings.

Her hands smoothed up his chest, over his shoulders and to the back of his neck. He drew in a breath as she smiled up at him. "Yes," she said.

Before he could think better of it, she pulled him down until his lips touched hers. Her body pressed into his. The bare skin of his stomach brushed against her soft skin. The contact shot through him like a bolt of lightning. His hands grabbed her hips and pulled her solidly against him as he took control of the kiss. She tasted sweet. He deepened the kiss and let go of all thoughts of right and wrong, friends and lovers.

The touch of her chilled skin burned through him. Her fingers clutched at his hair as she gave as good as she got from the kiss. No one had been this close to Sam in years—not just sexually, but in the way she accepted him. She didn't give him looks as if she was trying to figure him out.

Somehow she knew him. It gave him hope that maybe, somewhere inside, that little boy who would have slayed dragons next to her still existed. Maybe that was enough for whatever this was becoming. If it didn't feel so right and good, he would have pulled back and apologized. But the noise she made in the back of her throat blew through any thoughts of good deeds. He was willing to go to hell for this.

Chapter Five

So this was what all the hubbub was about. Nicole had been kissed quite a few times before, but they were nothing compared to this. Sam didn't just kiss her; it was almost as if he was trying to make her part of him. As if he couldn't get close enough to her, though you couldn't have slid a piece of paper between their bodies at the moment. And then there was the buzz of attraction that rippled through her, making her whole body hum with excitement.

He was warm from the sun, while she was still slightly chilled from the hose water. She traced his shoulder with one hand, down until she could rest her hand on his scar. She'd been taken aback when she first saw it. Somehow she'd built up in her mind that Sam was invincible.

That scar represented how very mortal he was and

how little time they had. What if he'd died and she'd never gotten to talk to him again? What if he'd never smiled or laughed again? Had he smiled and laughed before the surgery? His heartbeat was strong and steady beneath her palm. His heart flowed with life. His body was hard and unyielding against her.

It wasn't enough. She wanted more of him. Wanted the evidence that he was truly alive. That he was here with her. It scared her how strongly she needed him.

He pulled back, and his blue eyes seemed dark and mysterious. The different tones of blue swirled together into a storm of desire. It excited her and frightened her at the same time. This wasn't the Sam she'd known or even the one she'd started to get to know. It was as if she didn't know him at all.

But her body trembled beneath the touch of his palms against her bare back, and she wanted to know this Sam. What made him tick under that hard exterior? She wanted to draw out the boy she remembered and learn about the man he'd become. She wanted to make him talk to her about anything and everything and nothing at all. She wanted everything from him, and it would terrify her as much as it would probably terrify him if she spilled it all out.

His eyes filled with regret, and her stomach sank. *Please don't say it.*

"I shouldn't have—"

"I don't see why not," she said. Her breath caught in her throat as he released her and turned around. The wall of his back would intimidate just about anyone, but not her. She was done backing away from things because they were too hard to talk about. "You shouldn't have kissed me or you shouldn't have enjoyed it?"

He combed a hand through his wet hair and looked up to the sky.

"I don't think your answer is up there." She wrapped her arms around his waist, pressing her front to his back, and held on as if her life depended on this moment. She sighed from the warmth of the hug and rested her cheek against his muscular back. "I like hugging you. It makes me feel safe. There's nothing better than a hug even on a hot day. Well, okay, that kiss was definitely better—"

"That kiss shouldn't have happened." Sam didn't try to pull away, and she took that as a good sign, even though his words weren't exactly what she wanted to hear. "The heat must be getting to me."

"Oh, please." Nicole released him and walked around to his front, fully aware that neither of them had shirts on and that the bra she was wearing was soaked. The drops of water flowing down her cleavage had to be to her benefit in this situation, though. "Don't make excuses about the heat. You wanted to kiss me and I wanted to kiss you. End of story. Well…not really the end of the story, because I would definitely like to kiss you again."

He brought his gaze back down to hers. He was a wreck, but she could handle that. She was pretty much a wreck herself.

"You just broke up with your boyfriend and lost your job and home. Do you really think messing around with the guy next door is in your best interests right now?"

She let her gaze wander over the "guy next door." Her lips still buzzed from their kiss. "Does it make sense? Probably not, but life doesn't make sense. I'm not looking for a relationship or anything, if that's what you are worried about. I like being with you. I could use something uncomplicated for once in my life, and you are about as uncomplicated as they come."

Obviously he hadn't thought ahead to a relationship or at least that was the impression his expression gave her. "We shouldn't be having this conversation."

She gave in to her need to touch him and laid her hand over his heart again. "Try to deny it all you want, Sam Ward, but even you have to admit there is something here. Some strange chemical reaction waiting to happen."

He stared at her hand. "I'm not looking for pity."

She waited for him to return his gaze to hers. "I'm not offering it."

"What are you offering?" The look in his eyes made her stomach melt.

Mind-blowing sex probably wasn't on the table. If he got all bent out of shape over a kiss, he might have issues with her just coming out and saying what she wanted. The problem was, she was used to saying whatever she wanted. She'd never been a shy, wilting flower. But she also had never had a one-night stand. Before this moment, she hadn't thought she was wired that way. But with Sam, she'd be willing to try. Though if his kiss was a preview of what was to come, she definitely would have difficulty keeping her hands off him.

"I know we don't know each other as well as we used to." Her hand slipped off him. "I'd just like to leave whatever this is open." She smiled as a word occurred to her. "Optional."

"Optional?" He glanced around the yard. Maybe he'd finally realized they were standing half-naked behind his house. There probably hadn't been enough time for her father and the boys to get to the sale barn and back. But she definitely wouldn't want them to find her half-naked with the neighbor. Even if there was a reasonable explanation.

He walked over to their shirts and tossed her soaking-wet, dirty shirt back to her. "We should go inside."

She nodded and followed him into the kitchen. "Optional, like a choice we can make or not make at any given time. Like now. There's one shower and two of us."

His eyes flared with heat, and her knees almost completely went out from under her. Whoa, she was in trouble if just a glance could do all that. She was in trouble and terribly curious at the same time.

He grunted his dismissal before saying, "Go take your shower, Nicole."

She raised an eyebrow at him and gave him a look of challenge.

He grabbed a shirt and shorts from a laundry basket on the dryer and pressed them against her chest. "Alone."

Sam had been more than happy when John came back with the trailer while Nicole had been in the shower. But then John had invited him over for dinner. Even though Sam had wanted to avoid Nicole for at least a few hours, if not a few days, a man with cooking like his didn't turn down a free meal. So he'd reluctantly agreed to come over.

Now standing in the Baxters' kitchen with Nicole and Ethan working together to create dinner, Sam wasn't sure even a free meal was worth the feelings tumbling around inside of him. By now he would have thought that he was used to guilt and remorse settling in his gut. They'd both been his best friends for the better part of a decade.

Guilt over driving Brady away and remorse for never telling him about his daughter. Guilt over Luke and Penny. Guilt over not fulfilling his parents' wishes for him and his brothers. Remorse for letting them down. The emotions were heavy and so much a part of him, he wasn't sure he'd ever be able to let either of them go.

But Nicole… While part of him felt guilty and remorseful for kissing her, the other part of him was egging him on to do it again. The guilt came from betraying John. After all, his family's farm would have gone under years ago if it hadn't been for John's help. And what did Sam do to repay him? Kissed his daughter and imagined all the dirty things he wanted to do to her until he had her completely speechless.

Nicole glanced over at him while she stirred something on the stove. Her green eyes were filled with welcome and the happiness that always seemed to surround her. His pulse quickened in response. He was grateful that Ethan was here. He didn't trust himself to be alone with her.

What was it about her that drew him? Maybe it was that smile. It never questioned him and never made him feel as if he didn't deserve it. Her smile just was.

He'd break her if he tried to do anything more than be her friend. Just as he'd broken Luke and Brady. Her smile would fade and it would be his fault.

John came in through the back door with Wes. "Glad you could make it, Sam."

Sam broke eye contact and tried to control the heat that crept toward his neck at being caught staring at Nicole. Even though John didn't seem to notice as Sam turned to greet him with a handshake. "I couldn't turn down a home-cooked meal."

Not if he wanted to stay within the diet restrictions recommended by Luke and his doctor. Apparently microwavable meals were too sodium-filled for his heart.

"We've definitely benefitted from Nikki being home." John beamed at his daughter. "We'll all be fat until she leaves."

"I think you get too much exercise to worry about getting fat." Nicole wiped her hands on a towel and approached her father. She gave him a quick hug and a kiss on the cheek. "You boys would have to eat all day to gain weight."

John turned to Sam. "Why don't you join me in the living room? We'll grab a few beers and chat until dinner's ready."

Sam didn't dare look at Nicole as he nodded and followed John. He wasn't sure he could hide his lust for Nicole for five minutes, let alone an entire meal. He'd make damned sure nothing came from it. He knew what he was and what he wasn't. He wasn't the type of guy anyone settled down with, and he wasn't about to put himself out there to hurt someone else.

"Those were some good pigs you sent off." John settled into an armchair next to the old fireplace. "Surprised you didn't keep a few for next season."

Sam settled on the edge of the couch. His stomach tied itself in knots. There was a reason he hadn't kept any livestock. If he were considering a next season, he would have, but right now, he wasn't sure what he wanted. He wasn't sure he wanted a next season, but he couldn't let down his family legacy. He was well and truly stuck with no father to offer him advice.

John shifted in his chair and searched for the remote control. He had always been there for Sam when it came to the farm and advice, had worked this farm alongside Sam's father for decades. They'd grown up together. If anyone knew what his father would say, it would be John.

Sam swallowed some of his beer before saying, "I could actually use some advice."

"That farm darn near runs itself. Can't see how I can help, but go ahead." John turned on the TV. Some old black-and-white show played, but the sound was off.

Sam rubbed the back of his neck. "I've been thinking about doing something other than farming…"

"Sure, lots of farmers do stuff in the off-season. I know a few who work construction during the season, as well. What type of job are you looking for?" John stared at the TV.

"Not so much a job as a change of scenery." Sam glanced around the room, taking in the old cream-colored curtains and the brown braided rug. Everything had a slightly dulled, old appearance. It was a place to rest at the end of a long day. Sam's living room was similar in size and probably just as depressing. At the end of the day, at least John had his kids. Two young men to help until they could take over.

Sam didn't have anyone.

"You thinking of renovating?" John scratched his chin. His five o'clock shadow was wiry and white.

Sam took a deep breath, afraid to air his concerns outside his own head, but he couldn't make this kind of decision without some impartial feedback. Much as he loved his brothers and wanted their opinions, they wouldn't understand his difficult decision. They'd never had the responsibility of their family's legacy drilled into their heads since they were young. It had always been Sam's responsibility. "Our farm has been in the family for generations." Sam swallowed. "I always knew growing up that eventually it'd fall to me to run the farm, but I didn't expect that to be at eighteen."

John gave Sam his full attention. "You've done the best job your parents could hope for, Sam. Brady and Luke seem happy. You've got nothing to be ashamed of. That farm has good land, and between the livestock and the crops, you should be able to build it up into a self-sufficient, maybe even profitable, farm."

Sam met John's gaze head-on and said, "What if I don't want to?"

His heart pounded in his chest for saying out loud what he'd been feeling for a while now.

Wrinkles formed between John's brows as he leaned forward, all his attention focused on Sam. "What are you saying, Sam?"

"What if I don't want to be a farmer anymore?" It almost hurt to say the words, but it had been spinning around in his head since he woke from surgery. Luke had said if Sam didn't have the surgery, he would have died. Sam was alive. He didn't want to stay in this rut he'd been in for years. He needed something new in his life. Away from everything bad that had happened.

John leaned back as if the wind had been knocked out of his sails. "You could always lease out the land if you don't want to use it actively. Let the fields lie fallow. It would probably be best for the fields. It's been a while since your father—"

"What if I wanted to sell it?" Sam felt the weight pressing down on his shoulders. The weight of his family's legacy. The weight of disappointing his parents. The weight of responsibility that had been sitting there since he was eighteen years old. He'd been barely old enough to take care of himself and saddled with the responsibility of not only his mother's failing health, but also his two younger brothers and their family farm.

"Well, maybe Brady or Luke would take it off your hands. It's hard to let land go. Once it's gone, if you ever wanted it again, it would be impossible to get it back or find more like it." John wasn't saying anything Sam hadn't thought of before.

"Brady and Luke have their own lives. They wouldn't have time for the farm. Even if they rented out the fields, the upkeep of the buildings would take money away from their families." Sam rested his elbows on his knees and clasped his hands. "I just don't know if I can do it anymore. I want to be free to choose my life."

"Think on it, Sam." John leaned back and rocked in his chair. "If you are thinking about selling, though, I'd be willing to give you a fair price for the land. I'd hate for it to go into the hands of another weekender, tearing up the fields with his four-wheeler."

Some of the weight eased off Sam. Having the option of leaving it in John's hands, knowing that Wes and Ethan would someday own the land, relieved the stone that had settled in his stomach. The land needed someone who cared about it, not the man who had been forced to stay there.

"You'd be the first one I offered it to." Sam rubbed the back of his neck. "I'll have to get an appraiser to figure out the price, but I'd rather it go to you than anyone else."

"Appraiser for what?" Both of them turned at Nicole's voice. She stood in the doorway, looking back and forth between the two of them. "What would you rather go to my dad?"

"Sam's just thinking out loud, Nik." John stood as he spoke. "Is dinner ready?"

"Yeah. Wes is finishing setting the table." Nicole looked past her father, directly at Sam, who hadn't stood yet. He refused to squirm in his seat. Either she'd heard what they were discussing or not. It didn't make a difference.

"I better go watch that boy," John said. "He'll eat all the rolls before they get to the table." John ambled past Nicole without a backward glance.

Sam could feel her eyes digging into him, so he met them head-on. He had nothing to be ashamed of. It was his life, and what he did with it was his business.

"Are you going to tell me what you were 'thinking out loud' about?" She leaned against the doorjamb and crossed her arms.

"Asking your dad's advice on selling my farm."

Her mouth dropped open. "What?"

He knew she'd heard him and understood. Instead of replying, he stood up and made his way to the doorway, planning to pass her and go sit at the table. She stepped in his way. He should have known she wouldn't let him get that far. He could pick her up and set her to the side, but that had the potential to cause a scene he didn't want to have to explain to John.

"How could you even think about selling your farm?" She gave him a look that should have been stern, but on her it didn't quite come across. She was too sweet to be stern.

"Let it go, Nicole." Sam made an impatient gesture to shoo her out of the way.

"If you think we are done talking about this, you are sadly mistaken." Her lips set into a firm line, but she spun and preceded him into the dining room.

Her brothers and father were already settled at the table, leaving the only two open spots next to each other. He hoped Nicole would let the subject of him selling his farm go for at least the duration of dinner. While he didn't mind talking to John about it, he didn't want to get Ethan's and Wes's hopes up about him selling the farm to them.

John and he would have to come to agreeable terms before anything could happen. He couldn't just give away his legacy. Even to a stand-up guy like John. A slow burn started in his gut. He'd also feel obliged to offer it to his brothers.

Without the farm, surely he'd be able to find his own corner of happiness. Maybe he'd have enough to start over or at least pay his way through school. While Sam knew that farmland was going for high dollars these days, he didn't know how much his farm would be worth. But it should be enough for him to start his life over, somewhere far away from Tawnee Valley.

Chapter Six

A farmer without a farm had to be like a sailor with no boat. As she sat at the desk in her room staring out the window, Nicole couldn't imagine Sam as anything but a farmer. As a kid, it had been all he ever talked about. Hell, he used to brag that he would get to be a farmer and she wouldn't. Last night during dinner, the guys had kept up a titillating conversation about crop hybridization. She'd barely managed to not fall asleep in her mashed potatoes. After dinner, she'd tried to talk to him about it but couldn't seem to get him alone. Ever.

He was avoiding her. After that kiss and telling her he might sell his farm, if he thought she was going to just let things go, he had another think coming. After she finished sending her résumé to a few new job postings, she was going to go give him a piece of her mind.

One of the postings was exactly perfect for her minimal experience in forensic accounting, and it was a great opportunity. It was with a firm down in Atlanta. With the salary and signing bonus, she should be able to afford a nice apartment there and still be able to save for a house. She'd at least have her dream job and the chance at her dream house. Who knew? If she stayed there, she might find her dream man, as well.

She closed her laptop and pushed it to the side. Outside her window, the heat was coming off the cement in waves. The guys were all out in the fields working. She really didn't know what kept them all so busy. But she assumed Sam would be equally busy.

Except Sam didn't have help as her dad did. Maybe that's why he wanted to sell the farm. Maybe he couldn't keep up with it anymore. Even though her father could use the extra income from the land, she couldn't imagine Sam anywhere but here.

She stood, and her skirt swirled around her knees. This morning she'd put on a skirt and blouse out of habit. Her clothes weren't particularly suited for farmwork, and she'd need them when she finally found a job, but she really had to go shopping for work clothes at some point. Borrowing her brothers' flannel shirts that swallowed her whole had to end.

Last night she'd made sure to wash the clothes Sam had loaned her so she'd have an excuse to stop over. Not that she needed an excuse, but it was easier to face those fascinating blue eyes with something to say other than "Can we do that kiss thing again?"

She grabbed a pair of shorts and a T-shirt and quickly changed. Her hair went back in a ponytail, and she forced her feet into a pair of tennis shoes that had seen better days. Even though the clothes were older and less floral, she felt more at home in them than in what she'd worn every day for the past few years.

The transformation from tomboy to girlie girl had happened so gradually that she hadn't realized it was happening. Her mom had insisted on her getting "nice" clothes for school. Then, when boys had started noticing her, it had made her want to continue to dress nicely. Work had been another factor after college, and of course, Jeremy—his opinion had been very important to her.

He'd always turned his nose up at anything less than perfect. To him, she'd been arm candy. Something pretty to bring to company events. To her, he'd been a means to an end, that perfect life she'd built up in her head.

She shook thoughts of him from her head and headed out the back door and through the field. The heat had retreated a little, and with the shade from the trees, the walk to Sam's house was comfortable.

She climbed the fence and paused halfway over when she heard someone call a name. She tried to pinpoint the voice, but the wind blew it away. A white blur whipped out of a bush and jumped up on her leg and licked her arm before she could even think.

"Rebel, down!"

She met sad brown dog eyes as he obediently sat at her feet.

"It's okay. I like dog kisses," she reassured the dog.

Rebel barked lightly before his head snapped in the direction of his owner. Sam came up over the hill. Jeans and a T-shirt seemed to be his work uniform. Of course, he looked damn good in them. If his chest was any indication, he'd look even better without them.

Her cheeks flushed and heat rushed through her body as she thought about that kiss. She wouldn't mind a repeat performance, but she had more important things to discuss with him. Like selling his life away.

"He's too big to jump up on people." Sam stopped behind Rebel, who turned and returned to sitting position. Sam ruffled the dog's shaggy fur.

"Probably, but he's still a dog." Nicole finished climbing the fence and hopped down on Sam's property. "A dog is a dog is a dog."

He raised his eyebrow. "A well-trained dog is important on a farm."

She mimicked his expression. "So what are you going to do with your *farm* dogs when you sell the place?"

Sam opened his mouth and closed it. His hand was still tangled in the dog's fur. "I suppose they'll get used to family living, like Rebel's brother, Flicker, who lives with Penny and Luke."

"Seems like a pretty big change for a dog that was raised in the country." With her hands behind her back, she swung her foot back and forth through the grass, trying to appear nonchalant, when she really wanted to scream and shout at him. "I brought your clothes back."

He stared at the bag she held up. "You can put them in the kitchen. The door's unlocked. I've got to finish walking the fence before dark." He gestured in the direction he was going, which was away from the house. Probably hoping that she'd go put the clothes on the table and leave. She wasn't that easy to get rid of.

"Great." She grinned. "I'll go with you."

Sam shrugged. "Suit yourself."

He headed along the fence line with Rebel and her

tagging along behind. She swore the only reason he was taking such big steps was to leave her behind.

She stopped and yelled at his back, "You aren't going to talk about this, are you?"

"Nope."

"Maybe I'll just go home, then."

"See you later." He waved a hand toward her. He didn't even turn around.

She wanted to stick her tongue out at him, but it would be wasted. Rebel danced between her and Sam's retreating figure.

"Oh, go on," she said to the dog, who rushed off to follow Sam. How was she going to get through that thick skull of his? Yelling at him wouldn't do any good. He'd just stand there and let her shout and would do what he wanted anyway. It didn't matter that he didn't know what was good for him. She needed a plan. Thankfully she had plenty of free time to come up with one.

Sam Ward wouldn't know what hit him when she was finished.

Grocery shopping was a necessary evil for Sam. If he didn't go, food wouldn't magically appear on his table. And while some foods he could grow himself, there were some things that he couldn't. Like chocolate.

He opened the freezer case at the market and pulled out a premade meal. Surely he couldn't ruin this. How hard was it to pop this in the microwave? Surely it wouldn't burn. Maybe this one was low in sodium.

"Do you know how much sodium is in that?" Nicole was behind him.

He was surprised he hadn't noticed her coming toward him. His body usually reacted as if being jolted with a cattle prod when she was near. He turned the box over and saw the amount of sodium. If Luke were here, he'd tell him that was his entire sodium content for at least two days. Even though his cholesterol was fine now, Luke wanted him to keep it down.

Sam put the meal back in the freezer and closed the door.

"Why don't you just make it fresh?" Little Miss Optimistic said.

He sighed and turned to look at her, bracing himself. Her dark hair was caught in some sort of bun contraption. Her green eyes sparkled even under the harsh lighting of the store. She wore a sundress similar to the outfit she'd had on the first day she'd been home. Fresh and light, like the pixie she was.

"Surely a farmer like you has a vegetable garden." Her ever-present grin reminded him of how soft her lips had been beneath his. He cleared his throat.

"I have vegetables." He turned his back on her and headed to his cart. Before long, she'd start on about how he couldn't sell his farm. Too many people had tried to control his life, except him. He hadn't made a decision on his own in years. Everything had been about his parents and his brothers and what they had needed.

"Then why are you in the freezer aisle?" Nicole shifted behind him and opened a freezer door. "Throw them in a skillet and sauté them with a little butter and herbs and they'll be yummier than anything you can buy in this aisle."

"They'd be charred lumps if I did that."

Nicole came around him, looked up at him with wide eyes and grabbed his arm as if he'd just told her the worst thing ever. "You can't cook?"

"It's not like a disease." He shrugged off her hand. "Mom tried to teach me, but somehow it never took."

"But how did you get so big without eating?" She arched her eyebrow to indicate she was joking, even though her face was serious. "Cow lifting takes a lot of energy."

He could feel the slight tug of a smile.

"Uncle Sam!"

Sam turned to see Amber barreling down the frozen-food aisle at him. His eight-year-old niece launched herself into his arms without any question of whether or not he'd catch her.

"Amber!" Maggie, his sister-in-law, called out a moment too late as Amber landed against Sam. Sam let out an *oof* but caught her all the same. He'd never let her fall if he could help it.

"See, Mom, he caught me."

Sam set her feet back on the floor and unconsciously ran a hand through his hair as he looked up at Maggie and Brady heading toward him. Even though Brady was two years younger, Sam always felt like a fool next to him. Brady had been the best at everything: sports, academics and popularity as class president. While Sam had just been a farm boy in school, Brady had excelled and had escaped because he was younger, leaving Sam with all the responsibilities.

They'd hashed a lot of that out when Brady finally returned to Tawnee Valley. All that was in the past now. Except for Sam's guilt.

"I see that, Amber." Maggie smiled indulgently. "How are you doing, Sam?"

"Good." Of everyone he'd wronged when he was younger, Maggie had been the worst. He'd made sure she got money from Brady, but he'd robbed her little girl, Amber, of knowing her family. He'd made Maggie believe that Brady wanted nothing to do with them. He'd finally tried to fix it by letting her know last year that Brady hadn't known about Amber.

Brady's and Sam's relationship had always been competitive growing up, but when their mother died, Brady had needed to be as far away as possible, leaving Sam resentful and hurt and raising their teenage brother, Luke, all on his own.

"Hey there, Sam." Brady held out his hand as if they were at some business meeting.

Sam shook it because it was awkward enough without leaving Brady hanging. "Hey."

"Oh, my God, Brady Ward!" Nicole came out from behind Sam, where she'd been out of sight. Sam winced at being caught with her. How was he going to explain Nicole's presence?

"Nikki?" Brady squinted his eyes as if he were trying to see her as her younger self.

Nicole nodded and hugged Brady tight. Brady turned to look at Maggie as if to ask if this were okay. A burning sensation started in Sam's gut that seemed to grow the longer Nicole held on. It was one thing to force her hugs on him, but Brady shouldn't be on the receiving end of anyone but Maggie's hugs.

Finally Sam couldn't take it anymore and made an interrupting noise.

Nicole glanced back at Sam with a sly grin, but released Brady. "Is that Maggie Brown?"

"It's actually Maggie Ward now," Maggie said a moment before she, too, got a hug.

"Mommy, who is that?" Amber stood next to Sam

with her own little stern face on. Every now and then, Sam caught her making expressions similar to his. He didn't mind. She was a cool kid.

"You must be Amber," Nicole said. She came over and held out her hand to Amber. "I'm Nicole Baxter. I was your uncle Sam's best friend growing up."

Amber looked up to Sam for confirmation. He nodded slightly. She beamed up at Nicole and shook her hand vigorously. "It's a pleasure to meet you."

"The pleasure is all mine." Nicole held back her laughter, but it bubbled in her eyes.

"How long has it been?" Brady asked as he took Maggie's hand in his.

"Around seventeen years." Nicole moved next to Sam to answer.

For a moment, it felt as if they were a couple, and a little warmth spread within his chest. If he reached out and took Nicole's hand, she'd let him. She'd let him do a lot more than hold her hand, but what was the point? He'd just end up hurting her and ruining his relationship with her father.

He took a step away from her and said, "Nicole was just asking why I don't cook."

Brady made an awful face as if he'd just tried a spoonful of Sam's eggs. "Trust me. That is one thing that Sam cannot do. He doesn't cook food. He burns food into oblivion."

"That reminds me," Maggie said. "I've been meaning to invite you over for dinner. You should come, too, Nicole."

"Definitely," Brady said. "We can catch up, and Sam can remember what a good meal tastes like."

"That sounds great." Nicole looked to him. Waiting for him to say yes, probably.

He looked at Maggie and Brady, and they were both patiently waiting with expectant looks on their faces.

Amber tugged on his hand. "Dinner'll be fun. You can sit next to me."

Knowing this was a losing battle, Sam released his breath and met Brady's eyes. "What day?"

Chapter Seven

Maggie and Brady's home was an old Victorian house with a wraparound porch and lovely woodwork. Nicole could only imagine how much this house would go for in a large city. Tawnee Valley wasn't large enough, though, to support high housing prices. It was the type of town with only a handful of stop signs and vast amounts of land between it and larger cities. Location, location, location.

Nicole knocked on the old wooden door and clutched the bottle of white wine to her chest. It was only a day after they had bumped into each other at the grocery store. For some reason, she was more nervous about hanging out with Sam's family than with Sam himself. While he hadn't spoken of them much, she knew his family meant a lot to him. She also worried that she'd tell them Sam was thinking about selling the farm out of sheer nerves. Sam might have already discussed it with Brady, but knowing Sam, probably not. She didn't want to be remembered as the girl who caused a rift between the brothers.

"Nicole?" Sam's voice sent ripples down her back. She turned to see him climbing the steps.

Smiling, she ran a hand quickly over the brown skirt she'd decided on for tonight. "Hi."

He stopped beside her at the door. His dark hair was slicked back, but judging from the curl around his ear, it was just wet, not as if he'd actually used product on it. Warmth spread through her chest. Jeremy had always had a very styled coif. He'd hated whenever she tried to touch it. She liked that Sam didn't feel that way about the styling part. She didn't know whether he liked having his hair touched yet, but she was determined to find out.

The jeans Sam wore looked brand-new, along with a black dress shirt, rolled up at the sleeves. Unlike her, his large hands were empty. The dark shirt made his blue eyes seem an even deeper shade.

She swallowed against her heart in her throat. "You clean up nice."

He ducked his head like a little boy who didn't want to hear the compliment, but then he lifted his gaze to her. "You look nice, too."

Nicole couldn't control her lips from spreading into a larger smile. She nearly danced on her toes at the admiration in his eyes. She touched the collar of her white shirt. "Thank you."

The door opened, and they both turned to stare at Maggie as if she'd caught them doing something they shouldn't, which was ridiculous because they were just standing there. It wasn't as if they were making out, though Nicole would have been game. Maybe it was because when Sam was near, her hormones went into heightened mode. But he was over there, and she was over here, and while making out would have been awesome, she still needed to talk to him about selling the farm.

Maggie smiled as she pushed open the door farther. "Come on in. I almost didn't hear the knock in the kitchen. Brady and Amber took Flicker for a walk. We're pet-sitting for Penny and Luke."

Sam waited for Nicole to walk into the house before following her.

"It smells fabulous." Nicole could pick out hints of a roast along with the slight hint of rosemary. "I hope you like white wine. I've never been much for red wine, too dry for me, but I know it goes better with beef."

"It'll be fine." Maggie led them into the living room. "Why don't you two have a seat? I'll put the wine in the fridge and check on dinner. I won't be more than a few minutes."

"That sounds great." Nicole stepped into the living room, aware of Sam a few steps behind her, watching her. The hairs on the back of her neck stood up and her nerve endings felt electrified, waiting to see if he would touch her now that they were alone. To distract her rampant thoughts, Nicole glanced around the living room.

The room was nicely decorated. Pictures of Amber and Maggie with an older woman, who must be Maggie's mother, were on the end tables. A picture of Brady, Maggie and Amber from the couple's wedding day hung on the wall over the well-loved sofa. The room was warm with colors and memories. Nicole wanted to wrap herself up in the room and take it home with her.

Sam sat on the edge of one of the chairs, looking distinctly uncomfortable.

"Haven't you been here before?" Nicole said as she glanced toward the door to make sure Maggie hadn't come back.

"Of course." He leaned his elbows down on his knees.

She moved to stand in front of him until he looked up. "Okay, what gives? You look like you've swallowed a cup full of medicine and want to run outside to puke it up. This is your family. Relax."

He made a yeah-right noise in the back of his throat, and before she could question him further, the front door opened. The sounds that filled the hallway from the group that walked in were heartwarming to Nicole. When she'd moved to California with her mom, it had just been the two of them. No pets, no little brothers, no manly voices. Just them.

A white-haired mop of a dog raced into the room. With its resemblance to Rebel and Barnabus, this had to be Flicker. The dog sat at her feet with its tail wagging. As soon as she petted its head, the dog turned to say hi to Sam. When Sam didn't automatically pet him, Flicker barked once.

"Uncle Sam," Amber lectured from the doorway, "you know Flicker wants to be petted and won't leave you alone until you do."

Nicole watched Sam's face as a hint of mischief rose in his eyes and his eyebrow rose. The change was so abrupt that if she hadn't been here before it happened, she would have never known how tense he'd been.

Sam glanced at the dog and then at Amber. "Flicker needs to learn that not everyone is going to pet him."

Trying to get a better view, Nicole backed up as Amber walked into the room and petted Flicker's head.

"He's a dog," Amber said. "Everyone pets him."

Sam reached out and tousled the fur on Flicker's head. "There. Happy?"

"Yup." Amber twisted on her toes and beamed at her uncle. "Can I spend the night at the farm this weekend?"

Sam opened his mouth to reply, but before he could make a sound, Brady said, "Amber, what did I say about waiting?"

Amber rolled her eyes. "Wait until after dinner to start asking Uncle Sam to spend the night." She spun toward her dad before adding, "But if I wait that long, he might leave before I get a chance."

Brady gave Nicole a what-are-you-going-to-do smile. "Please wait until after dinner to ask. I'm sure Sam won't leave before you have a chance."

Amber nodded and gave Sam a meaningful look before walking out of the room, muttering, "He always says yes, anyway."

Nicole waited until Amber was out of sight before letting out the laugh that had been bubbling within her.

"I'm never going to get the hang of this dad thing." Brady shook his head and sat across from Sam. "I'd say sorry, but I'd be begging your forgiveness all the time with Amber."

"It's not a problem," Sam muttered and stared at his hands. And, just like that, Sam was back to being tense.

In fact, the tension in the room was thick enough to make Nicole think twice about talking. Not an easy feat. Too bad she didn't think twice often enough, including this time. Besides, it was ridiculous for two brothers to sit in the same room and not even make eye contact.

"I hear you have a new development in works for the town, Brady." Nicole leaned against the arm of the sofa, not wanting to sit fully in a chair. Both the men were intimidatingly tall when standing up. Somehow they managed to keep their intimidating nature even sitting down. If she were to plop onto the sofa, she'd feel like Lily Tomlin doing her little-girl act in the huge rocking chair.

Brady met her gaze with those famous Ward-blue eyes, but whereas Sam's eyes had an air of self-deprecation, Brady's had a confidence and assuredness that she was sure worked on most women.

"It's been a tough year," Brady said, "from project proposal to getting ready to break ground. We're hoping it helps with the local economy. The plan is to hire locals and train them for the new positions."

"Impressive. All this from the twelve-year-old who used to pull my braid and call me a pony." She gave him a reassuring, teasing smile.

"I was just jealous that Sam had a friend his age. Your brothers were four years younger than me. Of course, no one wanted to play with the little tattletales." Brady smiled easily. From the slight crinkles near his eyes, Brady appeared to smile frequently. His smile was so different from the smiles Sam gave her. Those were always hard-won victories.

She leaned forward as if she was telling him a huge secret. "They are still tattletales. Can you believe they actually tried to get me in trouble with Dad the other day? Just because I was standing still for a moment."

"You don't say." Brady glanced over at Sam, who

hadn't joined in and hadn't changed position. The smile melted off his face. "Are you doing okay, Sam? Do you need some water?"

"I'm fine."

"Are you sure? I can get you something to drink. Do you have your meds on you?" Brady started for the door.

The change in Brady was so abrupt that Nicole could only watch in stupefaction. Sam wasn't an old man who needed coddling, but Brady was treating him like an invalid. Sam, who had spent the past week doing back-breaking labor? Sure, he might need a drink from all the sweating he did, but he didn't need anyone to do anything for him.

When Brady took off, leaving her alone with Sam, Nicole didn't know what to say. Before she could even open her mouth—to say who knew what—Sam stood and, without looking at her, walked out of the room and out the front door.

The wooden door shut quietly behind him. Nicole stood and went to the doorway of the living room. Amber came racing through the dining room and out the front door after Sam. Nicole could hear Maggie's voice admonishing Brady in the kitchen. The words didn't matter and Nicole couldn't discern them, but the tone was telling. This wasn't the first time something like this had happened with Sam.

Glancing at the door and back toward the kitchen, Nicole felt like an outsider whom everyone had forgotten was watching their family drama. No amount of good humor or smiles would fake her way through feeling comfortable with this. Not that she could blame Sam.

No wonder he felt uncomfortable here. Here he was, trying to get on with his life, and Brady treated him as if he still needed to be in a hospital bed. Maybe if she'd seen how weak Sam had been in that moment, she'd feel the same, but she saw him as the man who was stronger and taller than any tree she knew of. Even thinking of him as that weak hurt her heart.

She was helpless to fix this right now. She was the stranger, the outsider. What did she know about their lives and what had happened between them? Who was she to poke her nose where it didn't belong?

The front door opened. The voices in the kitchen stopped midsentence.

"Jessica says that black-and-white cows make the best milk for Oreos." Amber led the way into the house with Sam trailing behind her. "I told her that was ridiculous."

"Because milk is the same from any cow?" Sam's tone soothed the rapid beating of her heart. He didn't sound as if Brady had broken him. Maybe for a second it had been too much and he'd needed space… She wanted to hug him.

"No, silly. Everyone knows that brown cows make chocolate milk and that is the best for Oreos." Amber stopped and giggled as she turned to face her uncle.

"Of course." Sam's lips lifted into almost a smile, which seemed to satisfy Amber.

"Dinner's ready." Maggie stepped into the room with Brady right behind her. "The dining room table is all set."

Between mother and daughter, they'd worked to calm the situation. Amazing. The men stared at each other for a moment. As if one wrong move would send Sam back out the door.

"Smells great," Nicole said and moved up next to Sam. "Shall we go grab a seat before it gets cold?"

Sam dropped his gaze to her, and his eyes softened slightly, causing her heart to do a little flip. "Sure."

Dinner was interesting and different from those with her family. Her mother and she had always talked about their days while they ate dinner when she'd lived at home. If her mother hadn't moved into a one-bedroom condo after Nicole graduated college, Nicole might have moved in with her instead of returning to Tawnee Valley. Her brothers and father took on eating like any other chore. When it was done, it was done. No excessive talking or stories shared.

Amber and Maggie kept up a simple dialogue with Nicole. Every now and then, Brady would add something, but for the most part, it was the women speaking. Sam ate silently. His gaze never quite met Maggie's or Brady's, and he spoke only when Amber asked him a direct question. Even then, his response might have been nothing more than a grunt. Nicole resisted kicking him under the table for his apathy.

It was nice, though. She could tell that the family cared about each other. It was comfortable and easy, even though there was the underlying tension between Brady and Sam still. She wished she knew the whole story. If they were fourteen again, Sam would have told her everything by now.

"Who's ready for dessert?" Maggie asked as she stood and started to clear the table. "I made pie."

"Oh, now, that's just cruel," Nicole said with a woeful smile. "First, stuff me full of the best roast and vegetables in the world. Then offer me pie. I'm not going to fit into any of my clothes if I keep coming here."

Maggie smiled. "I'm glad you enjoyed dinner. Amber insisted on helping to make the pie. Blueberry is one of Sam's favorites."

"It was a good meal, Maggie," Sam said.

Nicole glanced over at Sam before standing. "Let me help you clear the table. Maybe it'll help me burn a few calories so I'll have room for pie."

What she really thought was that Sam and Brady could use some alone time to work out their issues. But that was mostly wishful thinking on her part. She knew Sam wasn't about to become emotionally available to his brother and open up with constructive feedback. Maybe if Brady weren't so sensitive to Sam's surgery, it would be easier.

She followed Maggie into the kitchen. When they were out of earshot, she couldn't help but ask conspiratorially, "Is he always like that?"

"You should see him when Luke's around." Maggie gave a little smile while she started the water for the dishes.

"I can't imagine." Nicole grabbed a towel from a drawer to help dry.

"Sam's never been much of a talker..."

Nicole paused for a moment before she said, "Oh, I meant Brady. Being so concerned about Sam. It's not like he's an invalid. Besides, Sam is just being Sam." Nicole grabbed a plate to dry and almost missed the stunned look on Maggie's face.

Maggie shrugged and put another dish in the drying rack. "Huh, I guess Sam is just being Sam." They washed and dried in silence for a moment before Maggie said, "I know it's none of my business and feel free to say so, but is there something going on between you two?"

Nicole looked over her shoulder in the direction of the dining room, the plate in her hands forgotten for a moment. That was *the* question, wasn't it? There was something between them, but did it have a definition? She'd like to know the answer herself.

Shaking herself out of it, she smiled at Maggie. "We were friends years ago. I'm trying to regroup and figure out where I want to be in life. I just got out of a dead-end relationship and lost my job due to cutbacks. It seems like both Sam and I just need a friend right now."

"Sam could definitely use a friend. I've never seen someone who likes to be alone so much. It's like pulling teeth to get him to leave that farm and come in for dinner. I've dragged him shopping with me and Amber a few times just to get him out of that house." Maggie drained the dishwater. "Thank you for helping with the dishes. We better get the pie out there."

Maggie handed her a stack of plates, and Nicole followed her out of the kitchen. The fact that Sam was reclusive didn't surprise Nicole. She didn't mind that he didn't talk much, but usually with family, people felt free to open up. The fact that Sam was more silent than ever at dinner made her chest pinch. No friends. No family to open up to. No lover. Maybe he did need a change of scenery.

But that shouldn't mean he should sell his farm.

The pie was divine, even though Nicole was able to eat only half a slice. Amber cajoled Sam into playing a game of checkers with her while Maggie took the plates out to the kitchen. She insisted that Nicole stay put and make herself comfortable.

Brady stepped outside to take a business call. With everyone else occupied, Nicole watched Sam and Amber play in silence for a few minutes before wandering outside for some fresh air. Her mind swam with all the information she'd gleaned from this family dinner, but there were still holes in the puzzle that was Sam.

The night air was cool with just that hint of mugginess it got right before a good rain. She sat on the wooden bench and breathed deeply. It was still a novelty that fall was approaching. In California, the temperature was always around seventy and sunny. How much longer would she be here? Would she be around to see the leaves drop? Would she see the first snow? Or would she be gone in a few weeks if these jobs panned out? Would she have enough time to figure out Sam before she left?

Why was he so anxious to sell the farm and move away when his family was here? The tension between Brady and Sam had been very real, and it couldn't have been from when they were growing up together. They'd never been best friends, but they had gotten along all right. So what was it? Had there been a girl? Money problems? A fight over the farm?

"Hey," Brady said to her. His footsteps were loud as they hit the wooden porch. He leaned against the porch railing and tapped something on his phone.

"How was your call?" she asked.

Brady ran a hand through his hair. "As good as most work calls are. During family time, they usually call only for emergencies, which makes Maggie happier."

"Ah, the work call." She smiled. "Usually when Jeremy would get one, I'd get one shortly after. It seemed as if the world had an exact time for work calls—when you were off. The same with emails you couldn't put off until the next day." Nicole straightened her legs out in front of her.

Brady stashed his phone in his pocket and crossed his arms. The lighting from the street lamps was dim, and with his back to them, she couldn't see his eyes. Even his expression was hidden by the shadows. "What did you do out in the real world?"

"Forensic accounting." It was weird saying that. She hadn't seen many people since she got back, and most of the ones she ran into just asked if she was visiting. It had been weeks since anyone had asked her about her job. In California, her job had defined her status in her social life. Most people she met thought what she did would be exciting, believing she was figuring out how to incarcerate criminal masterminds with the power of money. Maybe it would be exciting once she got through the busy work.

"Nice," Brady said. The wind blew gently through the branches, scraping them against the sides of the house.

"Have you ever regretted your decision to come back?" She tried to watch his face for any change in expression, but Brady was a businessman through and through. She bet he'd have a great poker face.

"No. I have Maggie and Amber. I'm able to help Sam when he needs it." Brady looked over his shoulder down the quiet street. "It's not the hustle and bustle of London or New York, but it has its own merits. I don't feel as rushed as I did. I have a family again."

"Including Sam?" she asked softly. She wanted to know, but at the same time, she didn't want to know

what happened between them. If it had been a girl…
what if it had been Maggie?

"I was glad to be here the past year for Sam." He
didn't reveal anything, not even indicating if he thought
her line of questioning was strange.

"For his surgery?" she said.

"He told you?" At her nod, he continued, "For that
and for the farm. I left him with the burden of the farm
and our younger brother. I have some making up to do."

"You left him alone?" She kept her tone from sound-
ing accusatory, but she could tell how much Sam had
changed from the boy he'd been. Loss and years of isolation from family and friends could definitely do that.

"We had some words, and I had an opportunity that
had been too good to pass up. We were young and im-
pulsive. Everything happened so fast with Dad, and then
Mom got sick." Brady brushed his hand over his hair.

"Sam won't talk to me about it. Of course, he barely
talks at all. I guess I shouldn't be surprised. He hadn't
been a huge talker when we were kids, either." A dog
barked in the distance, drawing her gaze down the quiet
residential street. "We were a lot closer back then. He
could tell me anything."

"Don't feel bad. Sam doesn't open up to anyone that I
know of." Brady clasped his hands before him. "What's
going on with you two? He doesn't seem to know what
to do about you, given the way you were at the grocery
store and even tonight."

She smiled. "I like that. He doesn't know what to
do about me. I guess that sums it up nicely. I'm sure he
thinks I'm a mad top that just keeps spinning and spinning. I feel a bit out of control lately. He's my friend.
He's my happy childhood." She drew in a deep breath.

"Sometimes…" She glanced at the closed door. He was just there on the other side, so close, but so out of reach. "Sometimes I feel as if he's part of me. I know that sounds strange, but all my talking and optimism seems to be balanced against his doom and gloom. I guess I'm Winnie the Pooh and he's my Eeyore."

Brady chuckled. "I don't think he'd like to be called that."

Heat spread through her cheeks. "I didn't mean—"

"Trust me. I see the resemblance far too much. Maybe not so much with the 'woe is me,' but definitely lonely." Brady pushed up from the railing and held out a hand to help her up. "You should ask him about Amber and Maggie sometime. I think a lot of what he holds bottled up inside has to do with us. And what happened with Luke, too."

Standing in the shadows of the porch with Sam's brother being all cryptic made Nicole want to press for more, but she had a feeling that was all he was going to say on the subject. "Not even a hint? A point in the right direction?"

"If you want to know, you'll have to ask him. It's his story to tell."

She pressed her lips together. More puzzles. Now she just needed to find a way to make Sam talk.

Chapter Eight

At a rumble in the driveway, Sam glanced out the window into the darkened courtyard. The car Nicole had driven to Brady's pulled alongside his house. He sighed and set down the farming magazine he had been attempting to read. Putting his head in his hands, he waited for the oncoming storm that was Nicole.

Her shoes clacked against the concrete and then the wooden porch. She knocked on the door three times and waited for a moment. The screen door opened and shut. A chair scraped the old linoleum floor. Her fresh scent drifted over him like the soft winds of springtime. He braced himself for the questions he didn't want to answer or the admonishments for his childish behavior before dinner. He deserved to be berated, to be lectured about how to behave around people. He deserved her sharp tongue and harsh words. He deserved never to be forgiven. The sound of a bottle being placed on the table in front of him made him lift his head.

Nicole sat to the right of him at the table. Her dark hair was down as it had been for dinner. She still wore the simple brown skirt and blouse. Beautiful in its simplicity, the skirt followed the curves of her body like a lover's hand. The delicate scent of her played with his senses. Her face was passive. Her light green eyes indicated the beer she'd set down in front of him.

"I figured you could use that." She leaned back in the chair, not at all ladylike with her legs spread out before her, and took a drink of her own beer. "Long night?"

His fingers rested on the cold beer. His thumb played with the label, which had started to peel away from the glass. He wanted to be alone. Needed the reminder that this was his life. Alone. "Yeah, long night. Not really up to company."

"Me neither." She took another drink and stared out the kitchen window at the darkness beyond, not moving an inch.

He shrugged. What the hell. He took a drink of beer and relaxed back in his chair. Sooner rather than later, she'd get to her point. Nicole loved to talk. But as they drank, she didn't meet his eyes and didn't talk. She just sat there. With him.

A little warmth spread through his chest that only had a little to do with the beer. The crickets and katydids filled the night air with their unique songs. Somewhere a lone coyote let out a howl. A few minutes later, a responding howl disrupted the night. It was peaceful, and having Nicole here with him made him appreciate this moment, enjoy the empty night for a change.

She didn't look at him. Didn't expect anything from

him, at least not overtly. She wanted him to open up to her, but it had been a long time since he'd trusted anyone with his innermost thoughts. A very long time. Actually, it had been since he was fourteen...

"You didn't have to come over," he said when his beer was empty.

"I don't *have* to do a lot of things." She pushed her empty bottle to the center of the table and stretched her arms over her head. She closed her eyes and rolled her head around, stretching her neck. His eyes were drawn to her figure, and he swallowed, not knowing how strong he was to resist her. She was only a friend. That was the plan.

"I'm fine. You don't have to stay," he pressed.

Her eyes opened, and she tossed him a grin. "Seriously? Do I have to repeat myself? It's not a have. It's a want. Or rather a *don't* want. I don't want to go to my father's house, where my bratty brothers will be playing Xbox. Loudly. While my dad tries to tell me about the old days when farming was easy, as if it ever was. And if that gets to be too much, I can always retreat to my room, where my computer stares at me from the corner of the room, mocking me with its lack of new email and a competitive job market."

She leaned back in her chair again and returned her gaze to the window. "I'd rather be here. With you. Even if we just drink a beer or two."

Sam didn't know what to say to that. No one had just hung out with him for a long time. Even when his brothers had put him on house arrest post-surgery, Brady had been on his honeymoon, and while Luke had been here to help with the farm, he'd spent most of his free time in town with Penny.

Since he didn't know what to say, he said simply, "Thanks," and pulled two more beers out of the six-pack on the table. He set one in front of her and opened his own.

Tipping her head to him, she opened hers and took a drink. "I do expect you to talk to me eventually. You can resist my charming repartee for only so long."

He caught her wink and smiled.

"See." She pointed a finger at his face. Her chair legs returned to the floor with a heavy slam. "I've even gotten that elusive smile again."

"I have no idea what you mean." He chuckled and took a drink.

She wagged her finger at him. "Someday I'm going to make you laugh. And hard. I swear. It's my new life mission."

They sat quietly for a moment before she said, "So, you are going to have Amber this weekend?"

"Yes."

"What is that like? Obviously neither of my chuckle-head brothers has a child yet. None of my friends in California either, though one couple was pregnant when I left. I should at least email her to see how she's doing." Nicole started peeling the label off her bottle of beer. "She posts her progress to Facebook all the time, but you know how it is… Sometimes you want to have a personal conversation with someone. Connect. They were some of the friends that Jeremy got in the breakup. She was always super nice to me, though. We'd always sit and talk at parties. It's weird to think that people have to choose sides. I mean, they don't, really, but they do. You know?"

When she looked up at him expectantly, he nodded.

How was he supposed to know? He'd never been in a breakup that involved dividing up one's friends.

"There I go talking about my breakup. Again. You never talk about any girls that you've dated." She glanced up at him before returning her gaze back to the bottle. "Did you have a girlfriend like that? You know, serious? Or even someone you wanted to date and couldn't? Because she was with someone else or something?"

He reached forward and put his hand over hers to still her almost-violent ripping off of the label. Something was eating at her. She raised her gaze to his. Her eyes were a little glassy from the beer, but she was far away from falling-off-the-chair drunk.

"What do you want to know, Nik?" he asked softly.

She swallowed and straightened her shoulders. "Have you loved someone? Romantically?"

"No." No hesitation. He didn't take his hand off hers.

Relief flooded her eyes. What was that about? Her fingers twitched under his, but she didn't pull them away. Her face was an open book, and he could tell when she turned the page as something occurred to her.

"Do you think you can?" she whispered, as if even the crickets and katydids shouldn't hear their conversation.

"I don't know." He honestly didn't know if he was capable of loving someone. Or if he was just too broken. Could anyone pierce the guilt and remorse that enclosed his heart? Did he deserve to love after everything he'd done? He squeezed her hand slightly and let go.

"What happened with Maggie and Amber?" she asked. This time her intense gaze remained on his face, probably searching for any clues there. "Brady said to ask you. What happened with you and them?"

He took in a deep breath as his chest tightened with remorse and guilt over what he'd done. It had taken him a week of driving over to Maggie's before he had finally gotten up the courage to talk to her a year ago. It wasn't one of his better decisions. He'd hated himself for doing that to them. Was he really ready to talk to Nicole about this? What would it hurt if she knew? Maybe she'd finally give up on him once she realized how awful he was. Would she smile at him the same if she knew?

He'd miss her smiles.

He released the breath. "Maggie got pregnant with Amber and wrote here to let Brady know because Brady had taken an internship overseas. Instead of telling him or her, I gave Maggie some of the money that Brady sent every month."

He'd believed he was doing the right thing back then. But it had always sat wrong in his gut. He'd cut off his brother from his family. His mother would have been disappointed in him.

She seemed to absorb the information. Considering the words carefully.

"And Luke?" Not one ounce of condemnation was in her gaze.

Shoving his beer away, he rolled his head back. "His girlfriend, Penny, kissed me at his graduation party to make sure he broke up with her. I never told him that she collapsed into tears afterward."

"Oh."

He brought his head up. She hadn't moved. Her expression was still neutral. Not accusing but not pitying, either.

Her green eyes met his. "Why?"

Her question threw him off guard. "What do you mean?"

"Well, I assume at the time you had a reason to keep the fact that Brady had a kid from him. And that there was some logic to not telling Luke about his girlfriend. After all, you are a rational person. And while emotions can get the better of us from time to time, you seem pretty in control of yours. Were you angry with Brady or Luke?"

Brady had asked him why. Even Luke had asked him why Sam hadn't talked to him about Penny. But he hadn't expected Nicole to ask. He thought she'd just walk away and give up on him. But here she was, asking him why. Giving him a chance to explain.

"We were young, but that's not the reason. I was twenty-two. Brady was twenty. And Luke was eighteen. They both had new lives. Brady was off to London, following his dream, and Luke had a full ride to college. I was the one who had to stay behind. I was the one who had to bear the responsibility of the farm. I took on the responsibility of Brady's daughter and keeping Penny's secret so that my brothers wouldn't be trapped here."

Nicole moved to stand in front of him. He tipped his head back to look at her. Ready for her to slap him, to tell him what a mess he'd made of everything. She rested her hands on the sides of his face. "Like you were trapped?"

He didn't reply. He didn't have to. Maybe when he was older and wiser, he'd understand why, but for now, he just knew that she understood. He could see it in her eyes. In the soft sadness of her smile.

"I can never be forgiven for what I did to them." He didn't move away from her. He wanted to close his eyes, but he needed to see that she couldn't forgive him, either. It would be in her eyes. In her smile. In her words.

"Okay." Her smile was light and kind. Her thumb traced his cheekbone, sending a current of awareness arcing down his spine.

He must have misheard her. "Okay?"

"Did you want me to forgive you?" Her hands were warm against his cheeks. Her eyes were soft and not accusatory. Everything about her was yielding and accepting. His chest swelled with warmth.

"No," he said. He wasn't asking for forgiveness. He didn't deserve it.

"Then…okay." She lowered herself to sit sideways on his lap. "I'm not here to judge you, Sam. I'm not here to prosecute or defend you even. I'm just here."

She touched her lips to his and fire spread through his veins, along with wonder. From the moment he saw her in that tree, Nicole hadn't been what he expected. The tomboy he'd remembered had been replaced with a woman so optimistic and happy that even losing her boyfriend and job hadn't knocked her down.

Drawing her closer, he fell into the kiss, wanting to breathe in her essence and let it cleanse the darkness inside of him. To feel the warmth she filled him with eliminate all the cold corners of his soul. To have this moment with her and let all the corruption and darkness go for one night.

Her fingers tangled in his hair as she gave herself fully to the kiss. He felt her surrender like a kick to his gut. His body flamed hotter, but his mind resisted. This was wrong. Nicole wasn't someone he could just have sex with and leave the next morning without leaving a part of himself behind. As much as he wanted her, he knew this could only end badly.

He broke off the kiss and breathed deeply. His fingers gripped her hips. His body urged him to keep going. The battle raged inside him: the part that wanted her against the part that knew better. This was madness.

She opened her eyes. The light green was electrifying. Her pupils were dilated. Her lips were swollen and open in a small O, begging his mouth to take hers again. Against his chest, he could feel the sharp staccato beat of her heart along with his. She was offering him everything she was.

If he were a bastard, he'd take it and worry about the consequences in the morning, but he already carried too much weight of his wrongdoings. Adding this would break him completely.

"I think…" he began and swallowed as his body tried to force a lump in his throat to keep him from ruining this. "This isn't a good idea."

Her lips curved into a smile. "You're right. It's a terrible idea."

His chest pinched, even though he should've been relieved.

She stood, hitched up her skirt and straddled him on the chair. "Completely awful."

There in the kitchen he'd grown up in, Nicole pressed her lips and body against his. His excuses flew away one by one as her hands moved down his chest. The need to discover her mouth overwhelmed his need to keep her at a distance. He pulled her closer and was rewarded with a grateful moan from the back of her throat.

Her breasts crushed against his chest as she once again ran her fingers through his hair. The soft skin of her thighs felt like silk under his fingers. Any lingering thought of denying himself was stripped away when she wiggled closer to his hardness. His hands cupped her bottom under her skirt and pulled her even tighter.

It was too much and not enough. He wanted to continue to explore her mouth, but he needed to taste the rest of her. She was close, but not close enough. Definitely too many clothes. He trailed kisses across her cheek and down her neck.

"I want you, Sam." The words were tight and needy. She tipped her head back, allowing him access to her. He moved his hands up her back to support her as he leaned her back so that he could kiss down the V of her neckline. Her fingers dug into his shoulders, urging him onward.

As much as he didn't want to stop at this point, common sense started to ring in his ears.

"We can't," he said against the soft swell of her breast, kissing the skin even though it made him ache with need.

"We're adults. It doesn't have to—"

He lifted his head and met her eyes. "No, I don't mean that. It's that—" This was embarrassing. "I don't actually have any condoms."

She bit down on her lip. The wheels turned within her eyes as she tried to manufacture a solution. "What if we…" She glanced around the room and then met his eyes. "It's not like I'm not…"

Not ready to pull away entirely just yet, he said, "I'm

not ready to take any risks with you. We don't have to do this now."

Even though everything in him screamed that he should forego safety and take what passion he could, that wasn't who he was. Even with his new lease on life. He was the responsible one. As much as he'd like to believe he could take some risk with his life, this wasn't one of those moments he wanted to leave up to Fate. Fate had been a fickle bitch to him over the years.

"We could run to town…" she suggested with a shrug. She was fighting a losing battle. Right now, she had to know that she had him. That if he could, he would toss her up on this table and take her right now or better yet, lay her down on his bed and take his time to explore every inch of skin, every scar, every freckle, every imperfection that made her completely perfect. And if they waited…well, reason would seep back in when his blood flow returned to his other head.

He lifted her from him and helped smooth down her skirt, lingering over the curves. "It's late. We've both had something to drink. Driving in the dark country-side wouldn't be a good idea."

"Killjoy." She pouted and then smiled wickedly as something occurred to her. "We could do…other things."

Sam swallowed. He knew what "other things" they could do, but he couldn't guarantee he wouldn't be tempted to go further. Not with Nicole standing there looking irresistible with her hair slightly tousled and her lips swollen from his kisses.

Temptation in the flesh. He wanted her. He wanted to taste her and drive her to the edge of madness with need before watching her claim her desire. He wasn't sure he could hold back. Especially if she was as talkative in bed as she was out.

He tamped down the desire and tried to focus on something else. Anything but the beautiful woman in his kitchen offering herself to him.

"Why don't we just finish our beers and call it a night?" He lifted her beer to her.

"Where's the fun if you aren't going to try to take advantage of me?" She took the beer, though, and slumped back in her chair, clearly disappointed. He wondered if she felt as keyed up as he did.

He didn't answer her question as he took a huge drink of his beer, knowing it would do nothing to cool his overheated body. For a moment, he was tempted to grab his keys and head into town, grab what they needed and just get it over with. There was all this potential energy between him and Nicole, waiting to explode.

If they just got it over with…

She winked at him as she took a drink. "You really should loosen up more."

…he would hurt her. And that's the last thing he wanted to do. "Drink your beer, Nicole."

Chapter Nine

Nicole woke up with the feeling of cotton in her mouth. The sunlight behind her lids hurt her eyes. Either she'd been bit by a vampire last night or she had a massive hangover. Flashes of last night flittered through her memory in a tangled-up mess. Her last solid memory was of Sam telling her he didn't have a condom so they couldn't have sex.

Which had sucked. She'd wanted him so badly, even offered to take the edge off since they couldn't go all the way. As torn as he'd seemed, he decided against it. Probably for the best, since she wasn't sure she'd have enough control to stop at just fooling around when it came to Sam. So they'd finished off the six-pack and then got a few more from the fridge...and then blurs of colors, odd conversations about breeding cattle, and then...

She became aware of the fact that she hadn't driven

home last night. She forced her eyes open and stared at a strange lamp, strange as in not hers. It was fairly ordinary as lamps went. She pushed up on the bed, and a quilt slipped down off her body. She was still fully dressed in her blouse and skirt. This wasn't Sam's room.

She couldn't help the disappointment that went through her. Waking up next to Sam was definitely going on her bucket list. If hugging him felt wonderful, she couldn't help but imagine how nice it would be to wake up in those strong arms.

The room was almost bare in its details. It was either one of his brother's old rooms or the guest room or both. She struggled to the side of the bed, nursing her aching head. Her dad must be worried. She hadn't come home last night. Did she call him?

She reached for her cell phone, but it wasn't on her. It took her a moment to remember she hadn't been carrying it with her. It was probably at the bottom of her purse, which was probably still downstairs. Her cell was likely completely drained of battery.

There wasn't a mirror in the room, so she had no idea what type of mess she looked like this morning. Not good if the way she felt was reflected on her outside. No reason to dillydally, though.

Slipping her feet to the floor, she padded to the door and opened it into the hallway. It took her a moment to orient herself in the house, but she made her way down the stairs and to the only bathroom to do some repairs before she ran into Sam. As she washed her face, she recalled his lips pressed against hers and the waves of passion that had stolen her reason. She'd pushed him last night. The hot press of him between her thighs had been beyond temptation. Her body pulsed at the memory. She wanted him. All of him. All she could hope was that in the light of day, he hadn't reconsidered.

After a few minutes in the bathroom, she could smell something cooking. It smelled good for all of three minutes before whatever was cooking started to burn. She finished up quickly and went to investigate.

Sam stood at the stove, staring quizzically at the pan on the stove.

Her chest loosened and she smiled. "Good morning."

He turned to look at her. A soft smile played on his lips, and it eased the ropes that had bound her heart tightly.

"I see you weren't exaggerating your cooking skills." She moved forward and grabbed the skillet. "Here, let me." Taking it over to the trash, she scraped out the remains of whatever he'd been trying to cook.

"I would have eaten that." He moved out of the way, and soon she had some eggs and sausage frying and bread in the toaster.

"Maybe you are missing some sort of cooking gene." She grabbed a couple of plates from the cabinet. "Of course, that would mean that Darwin would starve you to death because you couldn't make your own meals."

"I get by."

She glanced over her shoulder at him and took in all six-foot-something of him. There wasn't an ounce of extra fat on that body, but it was far from malnourished. Healthy and fit and he'd felt so good against her. She cleared her throat. "Yes, you do. By the way, did I happen to call my dad last night?"

"After one too many beers, I called and let him know you'd be sleeping it off in one of the guest beds."

Thinking about what she'd wanted to do last night

in his bed, she blushed, but figured she could blame it on the heat from the stove. "Thanks."

She plated their breakfast and joined him at the table. Her knees loosened as she remembered how brazen she'd been. The alcohol could take only so much blame; the rest was on her. She'd wanted him. She still wanted him.

He dug into his food. Even though her head felt as if a steamroller had run it over last night, her stomach was more than ready for food. It wasn't her best effort for breakfast, but it was pretty darned good.

"I don't think we should do this." Sam put his fork down, but wouldn't look her in the eyes.

She grew uneasy. She'd moved too fast last night. She'd known that, but some part of her was sick of waiting. He was broken, but she was okay with that. She wasn't all that put together herself. She tried to brush it off. "Eat? Because even though I have a hangover, I'm pretty hungry."

"Not eat," he said. "This. You and me. It's only going to get someone hurt."

She tried to smile, but it was hard, and it probably showed. "I hope you aren't worried about me breaking your heart, because I know I have that effect on men—"

"Nicole—"

"No." She backed away from the table. "You're right. We're both mature adults who seem to have a problem connecting with other people. Just because it feels really good doesn't mean we should do anything about it."

He held his hand out toward her. "Nic—"

"No, you're completely right." She stood. "I'm too screwed up to be with anyone right now. I mean, what was I thinking? We're friends. I totally should have taken the hint the million times you said it before. You don't want to have sex with me. I mean, you want to— or at least your body wants to—but *you* don't want to."

"Please—"

"I won't bring it up again." She threw her hands up in the air, sat back down at the table and picked up her fork. "You don't have to worry about me. I'll eat the last of my eggs and go and when I come back, we'll just talk about you throwing your life away and me finding a job far, far away, so you won't have to worry about me trying to hit on you anymore."

She shoved the last bite of egg in her mouth and tried to force back the tears that were threatening to choke her as she swallowed. She couldn't look at him as she stood and took her dish to the sink.

When she turned around, he wouldn't look up and meet her eyes. *Coward.*

"See you later, Sam."

She half expected him to stop her. She half wanted him to pull her in his arms and tell her, *Screw everything. We should be together.* But he didn't. The screen door slammed behind her, and she left his farm.

It took Nicole a few days to build up the courage to go back to Sam's. Even then, she wasn't really ready to face him, but her dad had asked her to take some things over to Sam. What was she supposed to say? *But, Dad, the last time Sam and I were together, we were almost* together *and even though things could be intensely awesome between us, he just can't see it. And I'm afraid that if I get near him, I might attack him. Sexually.*

Nope, she couldn't say that, so instead she stood on this stupid porch, on the outside looking in through the screen door. How the hell did she get herself into this? How did she end up going from wanting a friend to wanting a lover? She'd always wanted Sam from the day she returned and fell out of the tree house. Besides, he was the one who'd started it by kissing her. So now that she wanted to be more than friends, why the hell couldn't Sam get on the same page?

It was not as if it would last, but a few weeks of down-and-dirty sex with a hot farm guy whom she'd crushed on since she was fourteen before she returned to the real world sounded awesome.

"Ms. Baxter?" Amber's voice called to her from behind.

Nicole put on a genuine smile as she turned to greet Brady's little girl, grateful that it had been her who snuck up on Nicole and not Sam. "Hello, Amber, is your uncle Sam somewhere? My dad has some stuff for him."

"He's out in the barn. He sent me to the house to clean up." Amber held up her dirty hands.

"I'll go give it to him, then." Nicole moved out of the way so Amber could go in the house. At least with her here, it should add just the buffer Nicole needed to not throw herself at Sam and beg him to take her. Something about Sam made her brain leak out her ears sometimes.

She walked across the courtyard and into the barn. Grease and gasoline assaulted her nose as she stepped into the workshop area. When she was young, she and Sam used to play hide-and-seek in this barn. Up in the rafters, out in the garage, in the cow-milking stands. Until Mr. Ward kicked them out. Then they would run around the yard or down in the fields until it got dark.

As she entered the garage, she could see Sam's feet

sticking out from under an old car. Memories flooded her of seeing her own father on the little wheeled thing that rolled on the ground. What was that thing called? She couldn't remember, but she remembered when he'd let her lie down on the board and roll under the car to see what he was working on.

"Hey," she said. Just like a girl with the worst crush on a guy who didn't want anything to do with her, she couldn't think of what else to say.

Sam rolled out from under the car. It really should have been illegal for him to look good with that much grease and oil on him. He had it smudged on one cheek. The dark blue coveralls he wore had seen better days. Given that they didn't really show much of anything, particularly the solid muscles that covered him, they shouldn't have done much for her, but her heart pounded a little heavier in her chest.

"Hey," he said, grabbing a towel to wipe his hands off as he sat up on the board. He had a wary expression and his tone was careful, as if he wanted to ask how she was. And she got all that out of a "hey."

Some days she wished she could be less talkative and more like Sam, just sit back and take everything in. He was probably comfortable with their one-word exchanges. But she wasn't.

"Dad wanted me to bring back these tools that you loaned him. He was really grateful. They are good tools. At least, I assume they are good tools. I didn't get to use them. Not that I wanted to use your tools, but if I had the chance, I'm sure your tools would be great." Her face grew hotter and hotter as she spoke.

"You can put them on the workbench." He gestured to the one behind her, but he didn't take his eyes from her.

She turned awkwardly and put the bag of tools on the bench. "So, I see Amber is out here. Is she staying the night?"

"Yeah."

She swore she spoke fifty words to his every one word, but that didn't stop her. "What do you guys have planned? Board games? Snipe hunting? Ghost stories? S'mores? How do you feed that girl when you can barely feed yourself?"

"She helps with chores, and then we watch some TV and go to bed early so we can get up and do morning chores." Sam stood and the air in the room vanished as he moved closer to her.

Breathing would be good, but with the whole lack of air thing, she just stood there. He grabbed a tool from the wall next to her head and then moved away. The air rushed into her lungs.

"Wait." When her brain finally caught up with what he'd said, she asked, "She works? That's all she does out here?"

Sam shrugged.

"Really? All the times we enjoyed roaming through the fields and building the tree house and hide-and-seek, and you make this poor girl work? Uh-uh, buddy, not on my watch." Nicole moved forward and took the wrench out of his hand. "Go get cleaned up this minute. We need to remedy this situation right now."

Raising his eyebrow, Sam eyed his wrench. "I need that."

She glanced down at the tool in her hand and then looked up at him defiantly. "No. You need to give that girl the memories she deserves of this place. The memories I know full well you are capable of giving. Because you gave them to me."

She held the wrench up and away from him for good measure. Not that she could keep it from him if he really wanted it. He was taller than her and outweighed her by at least a whole nother of her. But this was important.

"You can't shortchange your niece, Sam. She only has so much time before these things won't be as important or she just won't be able to make time for them." A reality Nicole had had to live with when her mother had moved her away. She set the wrench on the workbench and closed the distance between her and Sam.

"Please, Sam." She searched his eyes for his answer. "Trust me when I say this is important."

He reached out and touched her cheek with his fingertips. She held her breath at the simple touch, before he said, "I'll do my best."

Chapter Ten

"Pass me up the board," Nicole said.

Sam stood on the ground beneath their old tree house with his niece standing next to him, staring up at Nicole, this strange, wonderful woman, who he was starting to think was more of a force of nature than a mortal. He wasn't sure how she'd turned him around so completely.

He lifted the board and hefted it onto the platform.

"What can I do?" Amber asked.

"We're going to need nails and hammers and a lot of help if we want to actually make this a tree house instead of a sad platform in an old tree." Nicole's smile was full and uncomplicated. Her smile meant what it meant. There was no undercurrent of anything else. She was happy, so she smiled.

He hadn't wanted to push her in the garage of the barn, but he knew that there was something deeper to her desire to play with Amber. They'd both lost a bit of their childhood when she moved away. And he'd never stopped losing it from that moment on.

Responsibility had borne down on him until he felt crushed beneath its weight.

"I can go get those."

Before Sam could say anything, Amber had taken off at a run for the house and barn. Her excitement was palpable. He'd never known what to do with his niece. She'd always wanted to help with chores, so he hadn't thought to do anything else with her.

"We need a new rope or ladder or something." Nicole hung on to the branch and arched toward him from above.

"Be careful." Not that he wouldn't catch her if she fell again, but he'd rather her be safe to begin with.

She stuck her tongue out at him playfully before stepping back. "What do you think—ladder or rope?"

"I think you are crazy."

"Of course you do. But crazy is good." She smiled.

He couldn't help the return smile that spread on his face, because she was right. Her little bits of crazy were good and he knew it. He couldn't explain what happened to him when Nicole was around. She brought out a part of him that he hadn't felt in a long time, an impulsiveness that was bound to get him in trouble when it came to her.

He'd been worried that things would be awkward after the other night and the morning after. But just like everything else, Nicole seemed to let it roll off her and keep smiling.

"I got the tools." Amber came into view with a couple of hammers and a jar full of nails.

"Great. Get up here so you can help." Nicole winked.

Amber shoved the tools into Sam's hands and approached the tree with some visible trepidation. She studied it for a long moment before she began to climb. Like everything he'd seen Amber do, she did it with a thoughtful and careful approach.

Nicole had been right that Amber needed more than chores. She was a very serious child who needed some fun in her life. He couldn't begin to imagine what she went through. Maggie's mother had been battling cancer when Amber was born. Maggie had been the sole provider for her daughter and her ailing mother. The weight of that guilt shifted heavier on his heart.

No matter how many times he told himself he had done what he'd thought was best at the time, he couldn't give that back to Amber. He wasn't sure why she didn't hate him for denying her her father. He could only guess that Brady and Maggie hadn't told her. That secret didn't help with his burden.

"Are you coming up, Uncle Sam?" Amber had managed to make it to the platform. She looked down at him with a face so similar to his mother's that if he let it, it could break his heart.

"Yeah, Uncle Sam," Nicole said as she crouched down to get the tools from him, "are you going to join us?"

It was the question he'd been asking forever, it seemed. Should he join them or go away? He wasn't sure of the answer anymore. He'd been in the going-away camp, but with Nicole's open, smiling green eyes inviting him to join her, he wasn't sure he wanted to go somewhere she wasn't. It was frightening and exhilarating at the same time.

He hadn't felt strongly about anything for so long that he wasn't sure what to do with these feelings welling within him.

"Come on, Sam." Nicole held her hand out to him. "I'll even help you up if you need it, but really, you should be able to climb yourself at this point."

He could make an excuse and leave. Chores that needed to be done. Or he could spend a few hours in the company of his biggest regret and his biggest guilt. His heart was solid in his chest, reminding him that even though he'd been close to death, he was still here and should be taking these opportunities while he had the chance.

He met her eyes and said, "I'm coming up."

They spent the afternoon building the tree house, starting where he and Nicole had left off. Sam thought they had made fairly decent progress as the sun started to drop below the horizon.

As they climbed down the new ladder, Sam asked Nicole, "Do you want to join us for pizza in Owen?"

Owen was the slightly larger town nearest to Tawnee Valley and it had a really good pizza joint, where he and Amber would go for dinner when she stayed.

Nicole landed in the spot directly in front of him and tapped his chest with the back of her hand. "Ha. I knew you'd have a secret for cooking. I would love to join you after I have a chance to wash up."

"How about we pick you up in about fifteen minutes?" Sam said.

"Great." Nicole gave both him and Amber a quick hug before heading toward the adjoining fence line. "I'll see you soon," she threw over her shoulder.

He watched her go. He couldn't help it. She was everything he wasn't. She was bright and shiny like a brand-new penny. He'd been in circulation way too long and ought to be retired.

"I like Nicole," Amber said. She moved to stand next to him. "Do you like her?"

"Yeah." Sam looked down at his niece. "Yeah, I do."

"Cool."

They started heading for the house. They'd made it halfway when Amber asked, "Do you *like her* like her or just like her? Jessica says that boys and girls can't be friends because they always want to kiss the other one."

"And Jessica knows everything?" Sam raised his eyebrow, and his niece chuckled.

"I do watch TV, too." Because TV made anyone an expert, of course. Amber swung her arms back and forth.

Sam stopped himself from rolling his eyes.

After another moment of silence, Amber spoke up. "So do you?"

"She's a good friend," was all he was willing to discuss with his eight-year-old niece. She was right, though. All he could think about today was the other night in the kitchen and how he wanted to kiss Nicole more now than before. If he were smart, he would stock up on condoms. If he were smart, he'd stay far away from Nicole Baxter.

The problem was, he couldn't make Nicole stay away from him, and he wasn't sure that's what he wanted. He didn't know what he wanted from her. Staying away from her wasn't an option since they practically lived on top of each other and he needed her family's help with his farm. But when she was near…his pulse raced, his body ached and all he wanted was to kiss her until she couldn't find any more words.

"You need more friends. You smile more when you are with her," Amber said before she raced ahead.

Friends… He'd be even more alone if he moved away.

Could he leave all this? The quiet moments under the protective trees. His niece's laughter. Being close to his brothers. Above all, his mother had wanted them to stay together as a family. Sam had succeeded in bringing them back together, but he didn't feel as if he deserved to be part of this family anymore.

He didn't think they held grudges, but part of Brady must still hate him. Sam hated himself for what he'd done. He couldn't change the past, but he could leave and try to find some new peace. Something of his own. Something that hadn't been forced on him. A new life. A new beginning. New friends.

Amber giggled as Barnabus and Rebel greeted her, bringing him back to the present…and thoughts of Nicole. Nicole's acceptance of him with all his faults echoed in his mind. Her smile hadn't changed today. It was as open and inviting as ever. She didn't hold his past against him.

"I call bathroom," Amber shouted as she raced into the house.

He followed after her and cleaned his hands and face at the kitchen sink. The fields and barn drew his gaze out the kitchen window. A million what-ifs floated through his mind. What if he left here? What if he sold the farm and moved away from everything he'd ever known? What if he made his own way in the world?

"Ready." Amber stood at the door, waiting.

He grabbed his keys, and they headed to the truck.

The drive to Nicole's took no time. As soon as they pulled up next to the house, Nicole came out. She wore a pair of shorts with a light green shirt that rivaled the color of her eyes. Her dark hair floated around her shoulders.

His heart swelled in his chest and he worried that he was having an episode, but it felt warm and pleasant. What if he went with her when she left Tawnee Valley? What if she wanted him to? What would that be like? To wake up every morning to her beautiful smile? To her eyes the colors of his fields in spring? To her dark hair spread on his pillow?

"Hey," Nicole said as she took the front seat of his truck.

"Long time no see," Sam said. His lips tugged into a smile without him trying.

Her face flushed with pleasure, and her grin grew. He liked making her happy.

"Do you like pepperoni pizza? Because that's Uncle Sam's and my favorite," Amber piped up from the backseat.

"That's my favorite, too," Nicole said. She didn't look at him quizzically or question his change in behavior. She didn't look at him as if he had horns on the sides of his head because he didn't talk much. She accepted him…the way he was. "I'm so hungry I could eat most of the pizza."

"Maybe we should get two pepperoni pizzas, then," Amber said.

"Maybe just a large." Sam turned the truck around and headed for town.

An hour later, after a large pepperoni pizza and a stimulating conversation about school and the care and feeding of baby pigs, they were driving back out to the farm. Sometime after going under the viaduct along the way, Amber fell asleep in the backseat.

"Thank you," Sam said quietly. He couldn't think of how else to express his gratitude, even though the words didn't seem big enough to describe how Nicole made him feel. "For today. For helping with Amber."

"You would have figured it out yourself eventually." Nicole turned in her seat to face him. She glanced in the backseat before continuing, "If you left here, what would you do?"

Sam gripped the steering wheel tighter. The world stretched out before him. The possibilities were endless. "I don't know."

"What if you leave and you find out what you want to do is farm?" Her fingers traced the dashboard.

"I don't know."

"Do you know why you want to leave?" Her tone wasn't accusatory, just curious.

He turned down the road that led to his farm and her father's. How could he make her understand? "You could be anything when you graduated high school, right?"

She shrugged. "Yeah."

"What did you want to be?" He wanted to watch her face, but he kept his eyes on the road. Her expressive face was in his peripheral view. She was quick and would put things together, and when she did, it would show on her face. He liked watching her discover things.

"At first I wanted to be a scientist of some sort because science was one of my best subjects in high school. But I didn't really enjoy the intro classes, so I took some classes in the business school and found I was good at numbers." She stared out the window. A thousand miles away. What had she been like in high school and college? Did she like it? Would she change her experience if she could?

"When did you decide on forensic accounting?" He pulled into his drive but didn't go down to the house. He stopped next to the field of feed corn, put the truck in Park and turned off the lights. Finally he could turn and see her expressions in the dim glow of the dashboard.

She scrunched up her nose. "I'm not sure. I guess it was junior year. We had some professional speakers who talked about what they did for a living, and someone mentioned they were looking for more specialized accountants, particularly forensic accountants. Of course, he never mentioned that you needed auditing experience before you could move into forensic accounting."

He nodded and released his seat belt so he could turn to face her. "When I was eighteen, I headed to State to get a degree in agriculture because that's what my parents expected of me. I had barely settled into my courses before my mother called me to tell me my father had a heart attack. I got home just in time to watch him die."

Nicole reached across the truck and put her hand over his. Her warmth flowed through him. As much as he wanted to absorb that warmth and let it comfort him, he had to make her understand this. Had to make her understand why he was so messed up.

"I couldn't leave my mother alone with Brady and Luke. Especially when she got sick." His throat thickened, remembering how quickly she went downhill. "There was no way she could watch my brothers and run the farm. I had to leave college. I didn't get the chance to explore anything else. And then she was gone and Brady left for college and it was just me and Luke."

Nicole's hand tightened on his, but she didn't say anything. He checked on Amber, who was still fast asleep in the back, and swallowed the lump of emotion that had filled his throat.

"Luke was in trouble constantly. I knew that he was acting out. I knew he was in pain, but I didn't know what to do. I was angry and tired and too young to be the father he needed at sixteen years old. Too young to deal with the principal who had been my principal only a few years before. Too young to handle my brother getting into fights. Who was I to tell him what to do or how to act? When I wanted to do the same thing? When I was just as confused and angry?"

"I'm sure you did your best." Nicole's voice was quiet and reassuring in the darkness.

"I don't think I did. I was angry at my parents for leaving me with all this. The farm, the debt, my brothers. I was angry that they left me. I felt cheated and robbed of the life I was supposed to have. I did what I could to make sure my brothers weren't robbed of their choices. But I ended up taking away their decisions."

Nicole undid her seat belt and slid closer. She reached up and swept back a lock of hair from his forehead. She *tsk*ed and shook her head. "You are so willing to take the blame for your actions. Would you take a little credit, too?"

Her hand cupped the side of his face. "Look at your brothers. Brady has a family and a great job. He got the chance to live out his dream, and he managed to make it back to his family. What if he'd known about Amber? He would have had to leave his career to become a dad. He would have grown resentful with so many regrets about what could have been. Instead, he had the chance to choose his dream or a new dream with his family in it.

"And Luke is a doctor, and from what your family says, he's very much in love with Penny. They are both happy. Maybe they had years of struggle, but they are happy now. Why won't you let yourself be happy, too? You have brothers who love you. You have a niece who worships you." She paused, her eyes swimming with emotion, before adding, "You have me."

He glanced in the back at his young niece sleeping. He couldn't give Amber back those years with her father that he'd taken away. He couldn't give Luke back that time with Penny. In all those years between, he'd never found happiness for himself. He had worked and done what was required of him, but he'd never truly been happy. "I don't know how to be happy."

She leaned in with a reassuring smile. Her hand squeezed the back of his neck. "We can figure that out together."

Her words tempted him, even as his mind kept saying he'd find a way to ruin her life as he'd ruined his brothers' lives. But right now, all he could think about were her lips, how soft they were, and the sensations that slipped through him every time she was near.

He met her halfway and kissed her as if it were the first time and the last, savoring every moment, realizing that something had to change. Something would give eventually if he didn't find a way to let her go. A slight ache in his heart made those thoughts vanish. Reminding him that he almost hadn't had this time. He'd almost missed kissing Nicole, and that would have been the biggest tragedy in his life.

She pulled away and searched his eyes. "You deserve to be happy, Sam."

That was the one thing he'd never had, never thought he deserved. In this darkened truck, parked near a field, he wanted to believe her.

Chapter Eleven

"I want you to go to Atlanta with me for a few days," Nicole blurted out the following day. They'd worked in silence for at least ten minutes before she couldn't help saying what was on her mind. She'd thought to bring it up a little more gradually, but...

Amber had gone home, and Nicole had come over to help Sam with the chores he'd neglected the day before to build the tree house. They'd played that day, even though there had been work to do. It had been fun. Something she hadn't been sure Sam knew how to do. He seemed so much more serious than the boy she'd known.

Nicole had been bursting to talk to him. With him opening up to her, she knew it wouldn't take too much longer before she could convince him that right here was where he needed to be. He was a farmer through and through. He needed the land and the land needed him. He just needed to add fun to his life again, not move away, and accept his family the way they accepted him.

There was only one minor complication to her plan. If he stayed here, she might not get to kiss him again.

They'd kissed only that one time last night, but every time he kissed her, she wanted him to never stop. There was something untamed and totally not responsible about the way he kissed. His kisses flowed through her, sending jolts of desire coursing through her to pool in a hot and heavy ache. Just thinking about it now made her shift uncomfortably as that heat settled low in her stomach.

Her future would come soon enough. If she were lucky, there would be a lot more kissing before that happened…and more.

Sam raised his eyebrow at her, and she remembered her question. Atlanta.

"Not permanently, of course," Nicole said and set down the bucket of water she was carrying. "I'm not even sure if I'm going there permanently. I have a job interview. I got the call yesterday. And it would let you see the outside world. You said you haven't been off the farm in years, so come with me. We'll stay in a hotel and eat at good restaurants. We can go to the movies or visit old houses. Whatever you want."

Stay in the room and make out. Order room service during intermissions in a two-day sex marathon.

He set down the bucket of grain and ran a hand through his hair. His gaze went off into the distance, and she knew he was thinking about it. Maybe actually considering it. Her insides did flip-flops as he pondered. If he needed convincing, she was willing to offer whatever he needed.

"We could even get separate rooms if you want, though I'd be more than willing to sleep on the floor if you want to share. Of course, that's only if you are afraid to be in the bed with me. I'm sure we can put a wall of pillows between us. If you want to keep your modesty."

His eyes flared hot, and she got goose bumps on her arms. Her breath caught in her throat. She had a slight urge to step back at the intensity brewing in his eyes, but she didn't back away. Her body nearly trembled with anticipation of his next move. Would he kiss her? Hold her to him until she couldn't bear the thought of clothing between them? She swallowed.

"Or we can share a bed. And screw the wall of pillows." She clasped her hands behind her back and sauntered forward. Closing the distance between them with every step. Each step closer made her breath catch in her throat. It was his eyes, those startling blue eyes with so much heat in them she swore her clothes would burn off. "I wouldn't be opposed as long as you aren't a cover hog. Or have strange night terrors. Or startle when touched. Or—"

When she was close enough, he pulled her to him and kissed her, effectively shutting her up. Her heart felt as if it was only tethered to her by a string, so light and so full. When he drew her into his body, she rejoiced. Her body throbbed with the need for him to touch her. Her neck, her breasts, her hips. Everywhere. The background noise of the farm vanished until all she could hold on to in the world was Sam.

The only thing holding her to the ground was his kiss

and his arms around her. Finally. She sighed happily. She hoped he never stopped. When he lifted his head, his eyes sparkled in the sunlight. She drew in a breath, feeling the rub of his body against her expanded chest.

"Can I take that as a yes?" Nicole's voice had a breathless quality she couldn't have controlled even if she wanted to.

His eyes dropped to her lips. She could see the desire and the hesitation in his eyes. She wanted to wipe away the rest so that only the desire remained. She wanted that, ached for it.

"It's just a few days. Dad and the boys could keep up with your farm. They are just waiting until harvest anyway. We could play tourists and see the sights." When his eyes lifted to hers, she sucked in a breath at the heat. "Or just order room service."

A shutter fell over his eyes, and he backed away from her. *What did she say wrong?* She followed, not willing to let go of the contact yet. She put her hand over his heart, over the scar she knew remained beneath his shirt. It burned into her palm and her memory. She wanted to kiss it, trace it with her lips and make it all better, forget that he'd been that close to dying.

Time for a new tactic. "You are the one who wants to sell your farm and move away. Do you even know where you want to go? Do you even know what you want to be?"

He looked over her shoulder toward the house. "No."

"No, you don't know what you want to be when you grow up? Or no, you don't know where you want to go? Or no, you don't want to go with me?" She cocked up one eyebrow to mimic his earlier expression. It probably wasn't as effective when, while she cared what his answer was, she couldn't stop thinking of him kissing her again. Over and over again until they were both breathless. Until the outside world faded to a distant memory.

He ran his hands through his hair and dropped them both to his sides. "I don't know what I want to do or where. I just want to be away from here."

She nodded. When everything had fallen to pieces in California, she hadn't cared where she ended up; she just had to get away. She silently thanked her father for offering to let her come home. "I needed to get away, too. Things were complicated in LA. I knew I couldn't stay there. Why don't you consider this a trial run?"

Her palm itched to move from its spot on his solid chest. To trail her fingers up his neck and bury them in his hair while he claimed her mouth again. She wanted it to go further. She wanted his hands on her breasts and lower.

Her spine tingled. How many more kisses would she survive before he moved to the next step? She didn't need a fancy hotel room or even a bed. She was ready for him. She'd even stopped at the drugstore and started carrying condoms in her purse, so if they could ever get back to where they were in the kitchen the other night, she'd be prepared, and he wouldn't be able to deny her because of logistics. Not that she wanted him to have regrets about sleeping with her, because she couldn't imagine having regrets about him.

"A trial run?" He didn't move back.

For you and me. The temptation to move closer crawled under her skin, but she couldn't push too hard, which made her almost laugh when she thought of the guys who had pursued her. If she'd offered them what she was offering Sam, they would already have packed.

"You want to get away. Atlanta is away. It's a large city with tons of things to do. You could see how you feel about the city. Maybe go onto the college campus and get a brochure or talk to the guys at the fire station about being a firefighter. Whatever you want to do, we'll do it." What she wanted to do was him, pure and simple, hot and heavy. Maybe away from the specters of memories that lingered on this farm, she could manage to find that young man she'd left. At fourteen, she'd been worried about her crush on her best friend. She might never have worked up the courage to actually ask him to be more.

That would have been a shame.

If she'd been there to hold him through his parents' deaths, would she have been able to hold him tight enough to keep the demons at bay? Her poor Sam, all alone with everything weighing him down. Could she have held on to his light?

Nicole needed him to come away with her. "Please come with me."

He searched her face—looking for what, she didn't know. He sighed and released the tension in his shoulders. "I won't be good company."

She grinned, knowing she had him. Before he could even move, she wrapped her arms around him and hugged him. Her ear rested against his heart, and she squeezed him. His arms closed around her, and her insides filled with giddy happiness. "You won't regret it."

Sam already regretted it. The plane that was supposed to take them to Atlanta was small, and he felt like a giant walking down the aisle to their seats. It was little more than a tin can the pilot planned to fling to Atlanta with a huge slingshot.

He'd never flown anywhere in his life. When Nicole had said they were taking a plane, he'd asked, "Why can't we drive?"

"It's too far. Besides, we'll get there quicker this way," she'd responded.

Her hand touched the center of his back, and heat coursed through him. He'd let her book one room. She'd insisted that it didn't make sense to pay for two rooms. And she'd thrown the line at him again about them having seen each other naked or in bathing suits when they were younger.

They might have shown each other things when they were younger, but they hadn't known about what went on between men and women back then. It had been long before she left. They'd been little kids having a laugh. There hadn't been any sexual tension because they hadn't been old enough to feel it. Now he was constantly aware of Nicole.

This seemed like one of the worst ideas he'd ever considered. He liked Nicole. He liked listening to her talk, working beside her and, heaven help him, kissing her. By signing on to this trip, he knew he wouldn't be able to keep his hands off her. To have her beneath him and finally explore her lush body.

He'd managed to avoid being alone with her in the days leading up to this trip, but he wouldn't be able to avoid her in a small hotel room with only one bed. She'd told him all the two-bed rooms must be booked. If it hadn't been for the twinkle of mischief in her eyes, he might have believed her.

She wanted him as much as he wanted her. He wasn't

sure what held him back. That gnawing, nagging feeling that he wouldn't be good for her. That somehow he'd manage to screw up her life just by being a part of it. That if he finally had sex with her, he'd never be able to stop.

Every minute of every day, she roamed through his mind. Her hugs, her kisses, the way she felt against him. He couldn't focus on anything but the curve of her hips and the gentle slope of her breasts. He was a mess, and he couldn't fight his body's desire for her any longer.

He took his seat next to her on the plane.

"You look like you've seen a ghost." Nicole reached over and took his hand. "Are you afraid, Sam?"

Yes. He was afraid of falling for her. Of what harm he could do to her. Of destroying her beautiful, gentle personality with his darkness. When he didn't answer, she smiled gently and squeezed his hands.

"I know you haven't flown before, but it's really simple. You just sit back, relax and let it go. You can't control everything. You just have to trust that the people in charge have it under control."

Sit back, relax and let it go. If she knew the direction of his thoughts, would she still say that? There was no denying the desire between them. It was so palpable that it was a wonder the other people on the plane didn't feel it.

He was here on this plane with Nicole. Fully aware of where this was leading. Of what would happen once they landed. He would finally have her. But could he protect her?

Sit back, relax and let it go.

"It'll be all right, Sam." In her eyes, he could see that she believed that. "It's a quick flight and will be over before you know it. And once it's over, you'll wonder what all the fuss was about."

He stared down at their joined hands. Over before he knew it. That's what he was afraid of.

Nicole kept up a constant chatter that soothed him as the plane raced down the runway and into the air. It was a cliché, but his father had always said that if God wanted us to fly, He would have given us wings.

As much as Sam wanted just to let it go, he knew he'd let her down eventually. That she would blame him for the mess of her life because of something he would do, and he'd carry the guilt. He honestly didn't know if he'd be able to handle the day when her smiles for him went away.

"Sam?"

He turned to her. They still held hands.

"Are you okay?"

If he was going to lose her, he wanted to be with her. Even if it shattered anything good left in him, he would take the fall. For her. "Yeah. I'm okay."

Chapter Twelve

Sam had been acting weird since getting on the plane. Okay, so he'd been weird for a while now, but this was even stranger. Sitting in the cab on the way to the hotel, Nicole worried her bottom lip with her teeth as she contemplated the situation. It wasn't as if they weren't going to have sex eventually. There was just too much *stuff* between them not to.

She felt her body soften as she thought of the *stuff*. It was good stuff, better stuff than she'd ever felt before. She didn't want to stop and think about what that meant. She just wanted to live in this moment.

"What do you think of the city?" she asked him. His gaze was trained on the buildings moving swiftly by them on the way to the hotel.

"It's a lot."

She followed his gaze out to the concrete, glass and

brick buildings rising up from the ground. So different from the grass and trees they had come from. The farm had a serene feel to it. Down in the fields, it was wild and free. Nature at its greatest. Here, nature was tamed and confined to little plots within the concrete.

"It looks different than TV, doesn't it?" she said. "When it's up close and in your face? After a while, this becomes normal, and when you go to the farm, it seems so much more lush and green. The air smells cleaner, and it's like the weight of the world slips off my shoulders." She could feel the weight of these buildings. The grind of working fifty to sixty hours a week to get ahead. The struggle to find herself in a city this size with no friends, no family…and no Sam.

He squeezed her hand, bringing her back to the here and now. "It's different, but that doesn't make it bad."

"It's not just the buildings." She didn't know how to make him understand the current of need-to-have and need-to-do that ran through the city like a living energy, making you feel that you had to do the same thing day in, day out to get ahead. Get ahead of *what* was the real question. "It's the lifestyle. The rush. The materialism. It's hard to explain."

He nodded and returned his gaze outside of the cab.

The cab pulled up to their hotel just as the sun slipped below the horizon. Check-in didn't take long, and before she knew it, they were at the door to their hotel room. She took a deep breath. She was ready for whatever happened behind this door, but still she hesitated. Not over Sam. She wanted him. But over what she felt for him. What if she lost him because she couldn't connect with him? What if there was something flawed in her that not even an optimistic personality could fix?

Jeremy had never complained about their sex life, though it had become almost nonexistent in the past year. But his reason for leaving her was her inability to connect with him. Wasn't sex a form of connection? What if she couldn't connect with anyone? What if she was destined to become a crazy cat lady with forty cats and nothing else?

She spun around and stared up at Sam. "We haven't really talked about what's happening between us and what's going to happen in this room."

He held both their bags in his strong and capable hands. His dark gray T-shirt and jeans were casual compared with his newer pair of work boots. She didn't want to ruin this, didn't want to scare him away, but she should warn him at least.

"I'm not very good…" she started. The words jumbled up in her mind as she tried to organize her thoughts. How could she explain what she was afraid of when she didn't understand it herself? What had Jeremy seen in her that she couldn't see herself? What was so fundamentally flawed in her that she wasn't worth becoming a wife?

He raised his eyebrow and quirked up the side of his mouth.

She realized what she'd said and let out a nervous laugh. "I don't mean… Well, I don't know, I've never… Oh, God…" She covered her heated face with her hands. "I'm making a mess of this."

The key slipped out of her hand as he plucked it from her. The door lock made a clicking noise as he pushed open the door behind her.

"Inside," he said.

She peeked at him through her fingers. His reassuring smile sent butterflies rushing through her. She spun and entered the room with enough space for him to come in. Even though they weren't past the entrance hallway, the bed was in sight. The door slammed shut behind them with finality. Courses of shivers trailed down her back as she waited for his touch. She heard the rustle of him setting down the suitcases, and then his hands were on her shoulders.

She tensed; she couldn't help it. She'd been so sure earlier and so confident, but right now, when faced with that king-size bed… Maybe they should have done it back at his farm. It could have just happened, and they would have gotten that awkward first time out of the way, which usually wasn't that good, anyway. There was a lot of fumbling, and it didn't last that long. There was too much emphasis on doing it now… It felt too planned.

Instead of turning her or drawing her into his arms, he moved her forward, past the king-size bed, until she stood in front of the desk chair.

"Sit."

She did as he asked, and then he squatted in front of her.

He gazed up at her. "Nothing has to happen—"

"But I—"

"For once, Nicole, let me talk."

She opened her mouth, but then closed it and made the motion of locking her lips with a key and throwing it away. His blue eyes were kind and gentle. Her hulking giant on his knees before her. Her heart grew in her chest until she thought her chest wouldn't be able to contain it. She wanted him. Wanted this.

"We don't have to do anything. I want you and you want me, but it will change things between us."

"It doesn't—" She stopped at his chastising look.

"It *will* change things. You know that as well as I do." He waited for a moment, maybe wondering if she would try to interject again. She remained silent. Hoping he would say what she wanted to hear, and fearful that he would convince himself or her that sleeping together wasn't a good idea. If his kisses were any indication, it was the most amazingly wonderful idea. Maybe she was the only one who felt it. Maybe the connection she thought she felt wasn't real.

"I don't want to hurt you," he said.

She opened her mouth to tell him he could never hurt her, but at his look, she snapped it shut.

"We're moving fast. Even though we knew each other as kids, it's only been a short time since we've known each other as adults. We are headed in different directions. I haven't decided whether I can leave behind the property my family has worked for years, and you could end up anywhere for your job. I don't even know what I want to do with my life, and you've got yours all figured out."

"I don't." It slipped out, and she clamped a hand over her mouth.

He smiled and pulled her hand down. He traced his fingertip over the lines on her palm for a moment before lifting his gaze to hers. "The only thing I know is that this will end. Not today or even in a week, but you are going to find a job, and I'm going to have to make my own plans. If we do this…" He glanced over at the bed before returning his gaze to her. He took a deep breath. "If we do this, we can't take it back. We can't pretend it never happened. We can't stop ourselves from wanting something we can't have."

She wanted to ask him why they couldn't have it, but she'd promised not to talk. If he were leaving Tawnee Valley and she were leaving Tawnee Valley, why couldn't they leave together? But his farm... He couldn't sell it, even to her father. It was his life. He just had to be reminded of it. If she were to let him come with her to a large city, he would feel caged in it. He would regret his decision, and he would regret her.

When he didn't speak up, she braved a question. "Can I speak?"

At his nod, she slid down from the chair to sit on the floor in front of him and took his hands. Butterflies rioted in her stomach. She linked her hands with his, marveling at the size difference. Her small, slender fingers wrapped around his long, calloused ones.

"I don't want to regret never being with you," she said. "I don't know where life is taking either of us, but right now, we're together. Maybe it's all a cosmic joke, but I don't want to regret not being with you. I'm sick of waiting for things to happen to me. You make me feel things I've never experienced before, and I want more of it. For as long as I can. I want it all. I want you."

He cradled the back of her head in his hands. Her breath caught in her throat as he lowered his mouth to a hairbreadth from hers. His breath fanned her lips as he said, "Then you can have it."

His lips captured hers. She didn't think she could want him more, but the pulsing energy sparked by that kiss seared through her body, making her impatient and needy. She met his sensual onslaught with her own. Their lips parted, tongues parrying and thrusting until a small moan escaped the back of her throat and her core clenched in anticipation.

They both rose on their knees. Her breasts pressed against his chest and swelled into aching peaks. She was surprised their clothes didn't melt off their bodies with the amount of heat generated between them.

She threaded her fingers through his soft, thick hair, untouched by styling products. She could stay like this for hours, kissing him. As if swimming in warm water, she felt weightless and flushed all over. He didn't move his hands but continued his kiss, wiping away any other man's kiss from her memory. Replacing every kiss with his.

His thumb brushed over her jawline, and she gasped at the sensation. Every inch of her skin was a live wire waiting for his touch to spark. When he trailed his thumb and fingers down her neck, she trembled in his arms, and the hot, achy need expanded. She needed him to touch her everywhere. Find all the spots that would make her forget how to breathe.

As if he had all the time in the world, his fingers descended slowly down her back, leaving a trail of quivering flesh in its wake. When he finally reached the hem of her shirt, she thought she might die from the anticipation. He lifted his mouth from hers, and she gasped in a breath.

His fingers tightened on the hem of her shirt, and he rested his head against her forehead. His breathing was heavy. His blue eyes had darkened to the color of still water under the moonlight.

Why had he stopped? Had she done something wrong? Was he stopping? "Sam?"

He smiled, a wicked, tempting smile, and relief

flooded her keyed-up body, sending a fresh wave of heat over her. He wasn't stopping because he changed his mind. Her core pulsed in response.

In one motion, he took her shirt over her head and flung it off to the side. His shirt followed its flight shortly after. He waited then, his hungry eyes raking her body. Her breasts strained against the confines of her bra, her skin tingling with need, aching to be touched and to feel his warmth against her. He was shirtless, his chest a mass of muscles and unbroken skin with the exception of his scar.

Unable to stop herself, she reached out a hand, tracing over the scar with one finger. He hissed and she started to pull away, afraid she'd hurt him. His hand closed over hers, holding her hand against his chest, and she met his eyes.

"It doesn't hurt," he explained.

"What does it feel like?" she asked, holding her palm still against his chest. His skin was hot beneath it, and her own skin tingled.

"Like a jolt from a cattle prod." He rose to his feet, pulling her with him.

She followed willingly. There was something so right about being with him like this. As if her last puzzle piece finally clicked into place. Her heart beat hard against her rib cage. How could she feel this close to Sam when she'd never felt this way about Jeremy, the man she'd loved?

He tugged her toward the bed, still touching only her hand. The cool air of the hotel room caused goose bumps to rise on her heated flesh. His eyes settled on her pink bra, causing her nipples to tighten even more.

Now that he was sure of her, it seemed that he was in no rush.

"Sam?"

He raised his gaze to hers.

"Please touch me. If you don't, I'm going to die."

His eyebrows rose over his hot eyes. His mouth quirked on one side. "Such a drama queen."

"I said please," she protested. He drew her forward but didn't let her body touch him. A disappointed noise rose from her throat.

"Don't make me wait. I've been waiting for days. We can go slow the next time." She reached out for him and he took her other hand. "We have all weekend to go slow, but right now, I just want to feel you against me. I want you inside me."

His nostrils flared and the desire in his eyes made her believe she'd won. When she tried to move forward, he gave her a look that stopped her, reluctantly. They were going to play by his rules or not at all, was what that look meant.

He didn't say a word. He didn't have to. Her breath quickened as he reached toward her stomach. His fingers settled on the snap of her shorts. The backs of his fingers brushed against her belly, and she thought she'd burn to ash right then and there. He undid her fasteners and then slowly dragged the shorts down her body. His fingers brushed along her hips and the outside of her thighs and then her calves. Her knees weakened, but she managed to step out of her shorts.

He tossed them alongside their shirts and looked up at her from where he knelt on the floor before her. "Beautiful."

The word sent a different sort of warmth through her

body that settled in her chest. She stood before him in her pink boy shorts and pink bra, and he thought she was beautiful. His eyes worshipped her. How had she ever thought any other man was worthy of her attention?

His hand traced an old scar on the side of her knee. Barely an inch, the wound had healed many years ago, and she rarely noticed it anymore.

"Thirteen years old," he said. His attention focused on the tiny white line.

Her breath caught in her throat, and her pulse raced. He remembered?

"You fell from the tree house." His gaze moved to her face and riveted her in place.

Somehow she found the air to speak. "You carried me all the way to your house."

"Your tears soaked my shirt, and I couldn't think of any other way to make you better. I felt so helpless." His hand covered the scar, and his fingers brushed behind her knee, sending a bolt straight to her core.

"I knew you'd save me." They were best friends, but even then she'd almost hero-worshipped him. He'd been strong and one of the best-looking guys in school, and he spent all his time with her. It hadn't mattered that they weren't technically boyfriend and girlfriend. There was only one guy in Tawnee Valley for her. If her mother hadn't moved her away, he would have been her first. "I'm yours, Sam."

He didn't smile when he looked up at her, but that didn't stop her from seeing the pleasure on his face. It was in the tightness in her jaw and the crinkles next to his eyes. He stroked his fingers over the back of her knee again.

"I'm going to fall." She smiled down at the top of his head.

He stood. His body was close enough to her that she could feel the heat of him radiating onto her. "I already have."

Her heart skipped a beat, but before she could say anything, he lifted her against him and kissed her. Taking away words and thoughts. Bare skin pressed against bare skin, melting into liquid heat. She couldn't think anymore; too many sensations were flooding through her.

Her legs wrapped around his waist. For a moment, the feel of denim disappointed her. She wanted him to be as naked as possible, but then he pulled her more tightly against his hardness, and she gasped against his mouth.

He laid her down on the bed, and she kept him with her. Ready for the grand finale. She reached down between them and went to work on his button and zipper. He pulled away, and she whimpered.

She leaned up on her elbows to watch him take off his boots and jeans, leaving his boxer briefs on. The lines and muscles of his body were revealed. This wasn't a body developed by a rigorous workout program. His body was cut from good, old-fashioned hard work. His back was to her as he put the jeans in the pile. She slid off the bed, needing to touch him.

She reached out and traced his waistband with the tip of her finger. The muscles in his back rippled. She moved forward and pressed her front to his back and hugged him around the waist. What was a simple hug clothed had an erotic quality when her naked skin brushed against his.

He closed his hands over hers. "If you change your mind at any time—"

"Not a chance," she said, pressing a kiss to his spine. He smelled good, fresh. She wanted to remember every moment of this night. To seal it in a box that she could open when she was alone with her forty cats.

He pried her arms from him and turned. He was hers for tonight. A sense of urgency crept up slowly. What if this was the only night they'd be together? There was no discussion of a future together because it wasn't a possibility, but what if he decided that when they got home, they shouldn't continue?

He cupped the side of her face, and she leaned into his hand like a cat, needing him to touch her.

"It's been a while..." he started.

She smiled, teasingly. "Is this when you say it'll be better the next time?"

He laughed, a rich, full sound that captivated her. In his deep voice that struck the very core of her, he said, "No. I want you to understand that I'm going to take my time and do this right. I'm going to make love to you for hours. I want to touch you everywhere. I want to learn your body until I know exactly what makes you scream and what makes you sigh."

She shivered and backed toward the bed. Not an ounce of fear or uncertainty remained. She pulled down the covers and undid her bra, dropping it to the ground. His eyes feasted on her body, but he didn't move toward her. She took her time slipping off her underwear, letting his increasing passion feed her own.

Sitting on the bed, she looked him over, including the straining hardness contained under his briefs. When she reached his eyes, she held out her hand and said, "Show me."

"Lie down." He started toward her, and she reclined on the stack of pillows. Her chest heaved with each breath. Every time she'd imagined Sam taking her, it had always been hard and fast. And she'd had many restless nights thinking of Sam. She'd never imagined him as a slow lover.

He sat next to her on the bed. His hand stroked down the side of her body, and he proceeded to show her. Her body hummed for him like a well-tuned car. His hands, his mouth, his tongue. He worshipped her breasts until she burned for him. His hands left wakes of electricity flowing over her body and crashing in the center of her. Every touch, every kiss awakened a desire she hadn't felt before. A need that she knew only he could fulfill.

When he stroked her, the heat built in her core, settling there and churning with his every motion. He trailed kisses down her breast and across her stomach until he kissed the very center of her. Her back came up off the bed at the bolt of sensation that racked her.

She was teetering on the edge of something amazing. Her whole body tensed, waiting for something she couldn't begin to explain. She'd never been taken so high before. Sam moved over her then. His lips claimed hers in an all-consuming kiss that kept the fires burning bright while he covered himself with a condom.

Gently he spread her legs and entered her slowly. Just when she thought she couldn't take any more and would fall over the edge into passion-laden streams of happiness, he held still. Not letting her claim her pleasure, just yet.

She opened her eyes and met his. His pupils were

dilated, showing only a small ring of blue. He leaned down and kissed her. She felt so full of a cascade of emotions that she couldn't even begin to sort through them. Her body strained up against his. The ache was overwhelming. When he lifted his head, he held her gaze as he began to move.

It was intimate and erotic as he moved within her and she rose up to meet him, never breaking eye contact. She'd never felt so...connected to anyone before.

The Sam he'd been as a boy, her friend, her confidant, her partner, mixed with this Sam, new, complicated, a little broken. Her lover.

Her body tightened, and she arched up into him as she exploded into a million pieces. Like fireworks, the pieces fell slowly back to her body. Suddenly everything was so much crisper, and awareness of every nerve ending sparked through her. Sam had paused, waiting for her to come back to him.

He leaned down and took her mouth, stirring the ashes into flame. She gripped his shoulders, holding him to her, wanting him to take his pleasure after giving her hers. She'd never felt anything as intense as this. Never wanted anything so much.

He took hold of her hands, pressed them into the mattress next to her head and began to move within her, stirring the flames of desire into a blaze until the intensity was too much and she came again. This time he rose with her, bursting into the sky for so long she wasn't sure either of them would ever come down.

He sank on top of her, giving her a long, leisurely kiss that went on for days, stirring the ashes into a slow burn, before he rolled to his side. As he slipped away to take care of the condom, she stared up at the ceiling, waiting for her pulse to return to normal, wondering if it ever would.

"That was different," she said with a smile, before she turned to look at him. He returned and lay beside her, leaning up on his arm, just looking at her. She felt warm all over, as if she'd just stepped from a relaxing bubble bath. It was as if he'd known what she wanted before she knew.

He smiled, and it grabbed hold of her heart and squeezed. His smiles were more frequent now and worth the world to her. "Different is good?"

She nodded even though every muscle in her body was languid and fulfilled. "Definitely good."

His fingers trailed across her stomach, and aftershocks rocked her body. She loved the way he touched her. She loved his smile and the relaxation that she'd waited so long to see on his face. She wanted to make him smile over and over again until he forgot all the crap in life and kept only the pleasure. Kept only her.

Her happiness bubbled up unhindered, filling her until she laughed. "I take back my previous statement about good. That was amazing."

"I thought you said it was different," he teased. His fingers explored her skin with no urgency, no immediate desire to be fulfilled, just lightly tracing over her, stirring embers she would have thought would be happily burnt to ash right now.

"It can be different and amazing." She sucked in a deep breath as he cupped her breast lightly, his thumb circling her nipple. Hoping he'd say no, she offered, "I suppose you want to go out to dinner at a fancy restaurant."

"Does that involve getting dressed?" He leaned down

and captured her lips for a long, sensual kiss, reminding every nerve ending of the pleasure he'd provided. Of the way he made love to her as no one else had. And she wanted it all over again. She never wanted it to stop.

When he lifted his head, she took a few breaths before answering, "They do generally look down on nudity."

"Hmm." He took her breast in his mouth, lavishing it with attention until she was practically panting. His lips moved up to her neck and over to her ear.

"Room service, it is," she said. She pulled him down against her as he chuckled in her ear.

"As you wish."

Chapter Thirteen

The following morning, Nicole stepped out of the bathroom in her bra and underwear and went over to her suitcase, digging through for her interview outfit. Sam followed her and wrapped his arms around her waist, pulling her back against his front.

Her body sighed happily.

"I really have to get ready for my interview." She leaned back against him as his fingers splayed across her stomach. Reaching up behind her, she wrapped her arms around his neck. Cold drops of water dripped on her hands from the shower they'd just shared.

He didn't say anything. His fingers stroked upward to her breast, and she felt her knees loosen. Her eyes shut at the intense flood of heat that rushed through her body.

"How is it that I can still want more?" she mused

aloud. Her nipples ached to be touched beneath the confining bra. "It's not like we didn't just have sex."

In the shower. Her body flushed. In the bed. Always good. Sam had kept his promise. Hours of lovemaking, interrupted only by room service. But it was more than just a physical release. It was Sam, and he made it mean so much more.

He drew her arms from his neck and kissed the back of her neck. "Get ready for your interview."

She spun as he moved away and gave him the evil eye. "You were the one distracting me."

He wore only a towel slung low across his hips. Her insides clenched, wanting more. Wanting all of him. Including that broken heart of his. Her heart skipped at the thought.

"I would say you were distracting me." His smile was a slight crook of his lips on one side.

"You are incorrigible." The words probably lost their lecturing tone due to her grin. How could she not be happy? She'd just spent the most amazing night ever in the arms of this incredible guy.

He chuckled as he grabbed a pair of underwear and jeans from his suitcase. Her own suitcase was forgotten as he dropped his towel and slipped on his clothes. For a tall, well-built man, he moved with a grace that wasn't rehearsed or false. Her heart swelled.

He turned and noticed her staring. His eyes flamed hot, but he said simply, "Weren't you going to get dressed?"

She narrowed her eyes at him because it was his fault she couldn't get herself together, and turned back to her suitcase. She found her interview outfit— a cream-colored floral skirt that fell slightly below her knees with a cotton blouse topped by a cream blazer. It was hard to focus on her hair and makeup with Sam reclining in the king-size bed with only his jeans on.

If he'd been trying to make up for lost time last night, he was succeeding. She was pleasantly sore, which should have stopped her from wanting to have him again, but she did. Maybe she was making up for lost time, too. She'd never felt like this with anyone before, and it was more than a little scary. Could this be the connection that Jeremy had talked about? Did Sam feel it, too?

"You're welcome to join me in the bed." He set down the remote. His eyes were inviting, and she longed to crawl back into the bed and just listen to the steady beat of his heart beneath her ear.

Though she was more than tempted, she shook her head and grabbed some jewelry. "I have to finish getting ready."

What was happening here? He'd been right—they'd just done something they couldn't take back—but what did it mean? She could never regret last night, but she was going on an interview that could change everything. She could have a job and have to move to Atlanta... without Sam.

They hadn't even discussed what would happen when they got back to Tawnee Valley. Would they continue, or was this a one-time deal? Just this weekend? That wouldn't do. She wanted him for as long as she could have him. Her heart thrummed loudly in her chest.

"Sam?" she asked loudly from in front of the bathroom mirror. She spun to find him leaning in the doorway, watching her with a tenderness that touched something deep inside her. "We need to talk. I need to know what's going to happen when we go back to the farm. Are you going to avoid me again? Are you going to shut me out? Are we still going to have sex?"

"Slow down." He closed the distance between them, and she hugged him, resting her head against his heart, exactly where she wanted to be. "We can talk all you want when you get back."

"But…" For once she didn't want to tell him exactly what she was thinking: *What if they offer me the job? What if I have to move? What if I have to leave you?*

"Later." He leaned down and kissed her. A kiss full of promises of passion and laughter and happiness. When she wove her fingers together behind his neck, she never wanted to let go.

Nicole had left five minutes ago, and already Sam missed her talking. The hotel room was quiet, even with the TV on. He needed to do something. He wasn't used to sitting around. There was always work to do around the farm.

He flipped through the channels, not really looking at the shows. Last night had been wonderful and everything he'd imagined it would be. Nicole fit him. Her body, her smiles, her words, everything about her fit him. He couldn't think about her without his body tightening in anticipation.

When he'd warned her yesterday, the warning had been for himself, as well. He couldn't get attached. This was going to end. It had to. There was no option for them to be together unless one of them gave up something. And even if he gave up his farm for her, he would mess things up. It was what happened when he cared about someone. He wouldn't be able to live with himself if he ruined her life.

He clicked the TV off and pulled on his shirt and shoes, suddenly too aware of the direction of his thoughts and the regret and guilt they would bring forward. He needed to get out and see if he could find what he should be doing with his life.

Nicole's laptop sat on the desk in the hotel room. She'd connected to the internet last night and had told him he could use it whenever he wanted to. Maybe he should make a plan of where to go and what to do. Maybe a fire station or college or something. He needed more direction than just walking out the door and hoping the change he needed would smack him in the head.

When he opened her laptop, a program was already running. Open on the screen was a letter. He moved to close it when he saw his name at the top. *Dear Sam.* The date was recent, but the page number was in the four hundreds. He scrolled back and the dates got older and older, but the beginnings were all the same. *Dear Sam.*

The date on the first page was from a month after she'd moved to California.

Dear Sam,
I miss you. Do you miss me? Today, we finally moved into our apartment. Mom says I will go to school with some of the kids in the building and that I should go out and make friends, but I already have a friend. I have you.

He stopped reading. Were these the letters she'd mentioned writing but never sent? Curiosity coursed through him. Nicole had always been entirely open with him. Sometimes he wondered if she had a filter on her mouth as most people had. Feeling slightly guilty, he scrolled down a few months later.

Dear Sam,
I started school today. My class size is three times bigger than our class in Tawnee Valley. I don't know anyone. I miss you. We would be starting our first year as high schoolers. Is Megan still making googly eyes at you? I hope you don't end up dating her. I might have to stop being your friend if you do. Oh, my mom made me buy dresses. :P She said I needed to look nice for my new school. I said a new pair of sneakers would do it, but she made me buy girlie shoes.

He scrolled down more.

Dear Sam,
I think about calling you every now and then. Do you miss me as much as I miss you? I wonder if you even remember me. It's been almost two years since I saw you or heard from you. Are you driving that old car you and your dad were working on? Have you seen the twins and my dad? I miss them. Dad's going to try to bring them out here this summer, but he said that last summer. I wish he'd kept me instead of them. School is okay and I have a few "friends." They are nothing like you. You probably wouldn't even recognize me with my new dresses and fancy haircut. No more pigtails for me. :) I even put on makeup. I got asked to the winter formal. He's an okay guy, I guess. I wish you were here.

Would he have written her back if she'd sent these letters? Would it have given him hope, something to look forward to, between farmwork and homework? Once more he scrolled down, farther this time.

Dear Sam,

I know it's been a while since I wrote to you. I'm not even sure I'm writing to you anymore. I never send the letters. I miss you. I turn eighteen tomorrow. I've already applied for college out here. I thought about coming back east for college, but I got into Berkeley. Mom says you don't turn down Berkeley. I guess it really doesn't matter where I go.

I imagine you are going to the nearby college and getting your Ag degree like we always talked about. Going to college during the week and going home on the weekends to help out. I bet Brady and Luke are helping a lot more now. I thought about getting a teaching degree, but I'm thinking about chemistry instead. Mom says I should go into business because I'm good with numbers. I don't know what I want to do, to be honest. It's a little scary.

I was supposed to come back to Tawnee Valley after graduation and stay the summer. I was looking forward to seeing you and Dad and the twins. To see if our old tree house is still there. To see how much everyone has grown up. But I got an early admission letter and there is a program that runs for the summer that I'm going to take. Mom says it's good for my college career and will look good on my résumé. How did we get so old so fast? How can we make decisions that will change the rest of our lives within four years?

At least you have the farm. You were always so sure about everything, but I feel like a complete mess. I broke up with Bobby. He's going to New York University in the fall and I don't think it will work out. But that's kind of the story of my life. Boyfriends just don't work out. I miss you. I used to think that if I had stayed we'd have ended up going out together. You would have made a great boyfriend. Well, I have to go. If I sent this, would it make a difference? Do you think of me at all? Or am I just that girl you used to know?

He stared out the window at the city moving below him on the street. Did he think of her back then? Before college, yes. He'd remembered her eyes late at night and her impish grin and her ability to beat him in a race. He'd remembered staring up at stars on a blanket and talking about everything that passed through their minds. He'd remembered the urge that had been brewing within him before she left. The sudden awareness that she was more than his best friend. That she was a girl and he'd wanted to kiss her even back then, at fourteen years old.

When everything went sour, he'd thought of her often, wishing he had someone to talk to, but then he'd messed everything up and he figured he didn't deserve her, didn't even deserve to think of her, because he was not worthy of a friend. That he deserved his isolation.

Even though they weren't really letters to him and more of a diary, he scrolled down to the final pages.

Dear Sam,
You've changed so much since we were kids. Today you kissed me. And what a kiss! I thought I knew what a good kiss was like, but maybe it's because, with you, there is so much more to it than just a kiss. I know you've struggled and I want to cry every time I think

about you alone with your parents' deaths. I saw your scar today. You seem so young and healthy to have a broken heart. I wanted to wrap you in my arms and never let go, but I knew you wouldn't want that. I don't know what's going on between us. Maybe it's just remembering all the fun we had as kids or maybe it's because I thought I loved you for so long...

His pulse picked up, and his hands clenched. Because she thought she loved him? Did she still love him? A warmth spread out from his chest, filling him. But he shut it down; he couldn't have it. He couldn't have her. No matter how good she felt in his arms and how good he felt when she was with him. Even when they were just drinking beers and talking, even when they were covered in mud and laughing...

None of it mattered. All he could do was make the most of the time they had left. His gut clenched. She would move away, and he'd figure out what his next step would be. Without her.

It was a miracle that Nicole's feet were actually touching the ground, because she felt as if she was floating as she went to her interview. She should have been tired after getting only a little sleep last night, but she felt energized. They'd talk when she got back. Until then, she'd focus on her interview.

She stood in front of the massive building that was her potential future. It was a white concrete structure that jutted into the sky, effectively blocking the majority of said sky. Before she left, Sam had wished her good luck and given her a kiss that just about had her throwing down her portfolio and climbing back in bed with him.

Shaking off the desire the memory conjured, Nicole pushed through the glass doors and took the elevator to the seventh floor. She felt the familiar jitters that she always had when she went on interviews. The last time she'd gone on an interview had been a few years ago when she'd wanted something closer to what she'd trained for in college. She'd put in her years as an auditor, so she had some experience, but not in forensic accounting. It had taken time to find the right company. Most companies had had a few openings, but she wanted to specialize, and while her experience was good, it still meant getting in on the ground level. For a while she'd wondered if she were good enough to find a job.

She stopped at the receptionist. "I'm here for a ten o'clock with Mr. Bradbury."

The receptionist nodded to some seats. "If you'll have a seat, I'll let him know you are here."

Nicole had a few years of work experience in forensic accounting now, but this was a new firm, a new town. What if her previous experience didn't count for anything? What if she had the wrong experience? What if every time she went up for a job, a better candidate would be available? This was her first interview out of twenty jobs she'd applied for. What if it would be her only? What would she do with her life if she didn't have a job? She could always try straight auditing. It was where she'd started her career, but would it be enough? Would it keep her from wanting things she couldn't have…like Sam?

"Ms. Baxter?" A man in his early fifties came out of an office.

Nicole stood and held out her hand as she approached him. "Mr. Bradbury?"

He nodded as he shook her hand. "Please follow me."

After they sat in his office, he asked her about her experience and how she'd liked working in California. A half hour of questioning later, he offered to take her on a tour of the offices.

As they walked through the cubicle jungle, Nicole's heart pounded. This was exactly like her job in California. The cubicles had no windows, an opening, a desk and a chair. Everything was a dull shade of gray. No sunlight, no greenery, no fresh air.

"We're planning to make a decision in a week," Mr. Bradbury said.

"May I ask about the hours?"

Mr. Bradbury smiled, changing his natural, somewhat discouraging look to a pleasant one. "We strive for work/life balance here. Though there are weeks that are heavier due to client needs, we try to make sure no one works over fifty-five hours a week on average. Flexible hours are available for appointments and such. You'll be given an access pass to the office building for weeknights and weekends, if you choose to work those hours."

He said all this as if it would be the most natural thing to spend most of her life crunching numbers confined to a four-by-four cube with a laptop. If she hadn't been at her father's farm for the past few weeks, this would have been exactly what she would have expected. This was the type of work she'd been looking for. It was as if this position had been designed precisely for her. The excitement and enthusiasm just weren't there, though. Even as she thanked Mr. Bradbury for his time and told him how excited she was about the opportunity, it all felt false to her. Her words, his smile, even the receptionist.

She'd had fresh air and sunshine and green pastures. Time to enjoy life without rushing.

It hit her as she stepped out of the building and into the glare of the sun with the heat radiating off the concrete sidewalk. She'd had Sam.

He was the one who had made her transition worthwhile. If he hadn't been there, she would have been bored to tears within a few hours and frantically looking for a job, any job. Even now, he waited for her to come back to him. If she took this job, she'd have to let him go.

Her future stretched out before her. She'd find some guy and get married after dating for an appropriate amount of time. After a while, they'd decide to have children, and because she'd be of a certain age, she'd probably have issues getting pregnant like many of her friends. She'd eventually burn out on the crazy hours, or her husband and she would decide she'd be better off staying at home with the children, where she'd do freelance work or consulting to supplement their income because they'd overbought when they got their house and the children would be involved in all sorts of activities. And by forty-five, she'd be so burnt out that the things she used to want wouldn't make her happy anymore.

She stopped just outside the doors of the office building on the bustling street. The air felt thick. People buzzed all around her. Her chest constricted and her gut clenched. It felt as if she could barely breathe.

How had she lived like this before? How had she been one of these mindless drones, floating through life? No wonder she hadn't been able to connect with Jeremy. She hadn't been connected to herself. How could she, without blue skies above and grass below? Without the hum of insects and the calls of birds filling the air with a chaotic natural sound?

What was around her was what she'd been taught to want. What she'd worked so hard in high school and college to achieve. What if it wasn't what she wanted at all?

Sam flooded her mind. She struggled to take a deep breath. To ease the ache surrounding her heart. What would she choose when it came down to the wire? What would she want if she had this job in the bag? Would Sam even let her choose him?

In the end, would it matter? She glanced around. No one had even noticed her small panic attack. Maybe she needed to do some soul-searching on her own to figure out what she really wanted in life. Her heart tugged, and she realized she didn't want to waste one minute of her remaining time with Sam, lollygagging about Atlanta trying to find herself.

She'd rather find herself in his arms for the next few hours.

Chapter Fourteen

Nicole's card key in the door had Sam up on his feet and heading for the entrance. The lights were dimmed and the curtains drawn as he waited for her. He'd spent the afternoon trying to focus on finding a job or career that excited him. But every few minutes he found himself back in her document, reading her letters to him.

He was the lowest guy ever. These were obviously not letters to him, but a form of diary where he'd become a character. Someone to direct her thoughts at.

He couldn't stop himself, though. As he read, his heart twisted in his chest. He'd read about her first time in the back of a car that hadn't been as good as she'd been told it would be. He'd read about her meeting Jeremy and thinking that he was the one. How perfectly he fit the mold of what she'd been told to want.

He'd read about her sex life and how she'd wanted

more but was afraid to ask for it. He'd read about her breakup and her exit from the only life she knew. He was peeking into her secret soul, and he knew he shouldn't.

But he couldn't help himself. It only proved how bad he truly was and what an awful person he could be. He should give her her privacy, not linger over pages of heartbreak and failure and fantasy.

Those were the best letters. Ones where she'd written her sexual fantasies to him, her dreams. Sometimes she didn't name the man, but other times she used his name. It made him feel guilty for reading them, but he couldn't stop the pleasure from rising when she used him in her fantasies.

He'd love to make every one of those fantasies come true. But he shouldn't even have read them. He wanted every page to be filled with him and no one else. He wanted to be the one who made her melt and cry and sigh.

The door shoved open as he reached it. He'd been waiting for her, ready to pounce. Ready to make her fantasies of him come to life.

She startled as he pulled her against his chest and closed the door behind him. Then she chuckled. "You freaked me out."

He backed her up against the door and grabbed her purse and tossed it on the bed. Her portfolio followed. He pressed his body into hers up against the door until they lined up: mouth to mouth, chest to chest, hips to hips.

"Sam, what are you—"

He cut her off with a kiss, long and hard. His hands went down her sides and inched up her skirt little by little. He wanted to make this last, but he wanted her so badly. He wanted to fill his mind with her, take all her memories and make them his own. He wanted her body and soul and everything in between. He wanted to consume her and mark her the way she marked him.

He'd always longed for a wife and family. He'd let that dream go a long time ago. But Nicole…she made him want more. She made him want it all.

When her skirt was bunched between them, he slid his fingers into the sides of her underwear and pulled them downward. As he lowered them, he lowered himself, pausing to lavish attention on her breast through her shirt. Her head fell back gently against the door.

When he was on his knees before her, she lifted her feet for him to slip off her underwear.

Her voice was breathless as she said, "You threw my purse and portfolio on the bed. Maybe I should go and move them so we can—"

He leaned forward and put his mouth on her sex, teasing her with his tongue and lips. Trying to make up for him not being there for her for so many years.

With her letters, he felt he'd let her down because he hadn't been there to be her first. It wasn't rational, but it didn't stop him from having wanted to be her first tentative kiss and to have been the one to bring her to immeasurable heights in the back of his car, so losing her virginity would have been perfect.

He focused on her now, the sensual woman she'd become.

Her breathing quickened with his every movement. Her hands splayed against the door for support. He cupped her bottom to help keep her upright. He wanted to burn this into her memory and his. He wanted no one to ever make her feel the way he did. If he couldn't have her, he wanted her to continue to write to him in her diary when she was married and every fantasy to feature him.

When she cried out her release, he stood and made short work of a condom before entering her. She clutched at his shoulders and opened her liquid green eyes to meet his. Her breathing hitched as he entered.

When she opened her mouth to speak, he leaned in and claimed her mouth. He didn't want her words. He wanted the unspoken. The emotions and intense feelings that words could never explain. Their bodies moved together as he teased her mouth with his tongue. He wanted to go for the rest of the day and the rest of the night, to give her something to write in that damned document of hers. But as her body clenched down on his and she went rigid in his grip, he lost it. No amount of control could keep him from riding out the wave with her.

As she went limp against him, he gathered her to him like the most fragile, precious thing in the world.

"Wow," she breathed out. "If I got greeted that way every time I walked in a room, I'd be a very happy lady."

Her smile was crooked and goofy. He kissed the corners of her lips, loving that smile.

"If anyone else greets you that way, I'll need his name and address." He tried to maintain a teasing tone, but even he couldn't deny the possessiveness in that statement.

"Yes, sir." She tightened her arms around his neck and sighed happily. "I swear I could sleep right here forever."

He chuckled. "Against the door?"

"No." She looked up at him. "With the sound of your heartbeat beneath my ear. With you."

His chest filled with warmth. Instead of responding and making a fool of himself, he eased her down and slipped into the bathroom to take care of the condom. When he returned, she was still leaning against the door with that crazy little smile playing on her lips.

"You know, I used to fantasize about this, but my fantasies definitely don't live up to the reality." She stayed still as if her whole body was weighted down. "I definitely think you've given me upgraded fantasy fodder."

"Good." He lifted her into his arms. She didn't need to know that he'd read that particular fantasy and several others. She snuggled against his chest, completely trusting, completely open. He was an ass.

He set her on the bed as if she was made of porcelain. Picking up her purse and portfolio, he moved them to the desk before joining her on the bed.

"Sam?" she asked quietly. Her fingers played with the neckline of his T-shirt while he trailed his fingers down over her body. Memorizing every dip, every curve.

"Hmm?"

She met his eyes. "Can we keep doing this until I have to leave?"

Wanting to avoid her question, knowing he was the worst person ever and she shouldn't want to be with him at all, he asked, "Lying in the hotel room? Probably only until checkout."

She pushed up on her elbows and gave him one of those you've-got-to-be-kidding-me looks. "You know what I mean. I don't know how long I'm going to be in Tawnee Valley, but I want to spend my time with you while I'm there."

"You seem to always be with me anyway." He slid his hand beneath her shirt and across the smooth skin of her stomach, loving the way the muscles contracted under his fingertips.

"I still want to drink beers and talk." She sucked in a breath as his hand moved higher. "I'd just prefer to do it naked."

His mind was slowly losing the ability to think as his blood flowed to other parts of his body. "You know that when you go, I can't go with you."

"I know that. You have the farm and family in Tawnee Valley. But I could come back and visit." Her voice had a hopeful edge to it at the end.

"No, you won't. Besides, I might not be there." He leaned down and brushed his lips over hers. "You'll get a great job and be so busy you won't think about me."

"No, I won't—"

"Or some other man will catch your eye." He unbuttoned her blouse and leaned down to kiss the swells of her breasts. "And you'll forget all about me."

She captured his face in her hands and brought him up until they were eye to eye. "I have never and will never forget you, Sam."

There was no playing in her eyes, and he knew this. He'd read it in her letters. He'd felt it with his body. There was a part of him that would always belong to Nicole, too.

"I love you, Sam."

He couldn't stop her. He'd thought about interrupting her as soon as the word *I* left her mouth, but he couldn't get around the lump in his throat. He wanted to tell her no, she didn't. He wanted to laugh it off, but he couldn't.

She pulled his face down to hers and kissed him. "I love you."

And he let her say it, did nothing to discourage it, because he wanted it. He wanted her to love him. Hell, he was damned already. What was one more thing to feel guilty over, to regret?

He couldn't make himself say the words back. He didn't even know if he was capable of love anymore, but he could show her what she meant to him. So he kissed her and gave her pleasure after pleasure. He'd keep her for as long as he could, and then he'd let her go and watch his heart leave with her.

Nicole wished she'd said she loved Sam every day they'd been together. Maybe that had been the key to opening him up. The airplane ride home was uneventful, and she'd kept up a light conversation. Her body was wonderfully sore but still ached for more.

They were in Sam's truck on the way back to the farm. No wonder she couldn't connect with her other boyfriends. In her heart, she'd always been Sam's. And now he knew. She should be upset that he hadn't said it back. But she wasn't.

If any of her other boyfriends had clammed up and just had sex with her, she probably would have kicked them out. But with Sam…it was so much more than sex. He made love to her. He was never good with words, but when he made love to her…she knew. She glowed just thinking about it.

She let her gaze sweep over his face. "We haven't discussed the sleeping arrangements yet."

He jerked a little, and his wheels went over the line onto the rumble strip. She couldn't help but smile as he got the truck back on the road.

He cleared his throat. "Sleeping arrangements."

She smiled, feeling mischievous while she watched his face for his very predictable reactions. The only place he was unpredictable for her was in bed, or the shower, or against the wall or door, or in a chair. She was beginning to look everywhere for possibilities.

"Well, I like to sleep, and I definitely appreciate you keeping me up all night, so there is that…"

"You're staying with your father." It was a simple statement that apparently was supposed to tell her the correct answer to her question.

"So I'm supposed to sneak out at all hours of the night and traipse across the fields in my black satin nightie that barely covers my panties so that you can feel comfortable knowing that my dad doesn't think I'm having sex with you."

They were almost to the turnoff for his farm when he took a side road instead. She didn't know these back roads as Sam did; maybe he knew a shortcut.

"You know when I did that thing you really liked last night?" she asked. "That takes patience and energy. If I'm exerting myself going from my place to yours, I won't be able to do that thing. I did enjoy doing that thing."

Within moments, he pulled into a small grove of trees along a gravel road. He put the truck in Park and rubbed his hand down his face. His voice was filled with exasperation when he asked, "Are you trying to get us killed?"

She rolled her eyes to the ceiling at his uncharacteristic melodrama. "Dad isn't as old-fashioned as you think. He definitely wouldn't kill us."

Sam undid his seat belt and reached over to undo hers.

"If anything, he would be happy because you're such a hard worker. Wha—" She squeaked as he pulled her across his lap so that she straddled him.

"If I were the type of man to hit a woman, I'd pull you across my lap and spank you."

She flushed in anticipation and giggled. "I have been rather naughty."

He raised his eyebrow at her. Thank goodness she'd worn a skirt today as she pressed against his hardness with only her panties and his jeans in the way. She moved a little against him, loving the feel of him against her.

"While I'm driving," he began his lecture, but at the same time he was undoing his jeans. Her breath caught and she felt herself go liquid at the brush of his knuckles. "You are not to mention beds, black nighties, black panties and, most of all, sex."

His hand rubbed against her until she started moving to the rhythm he set. He put on a condom and pulled her underwear to the side. As he eased into her, he said, "It's not safe for the driver to have a raging hard-on while trying to drive."

She sighed as she pressed lower on him until they were fully connected, and started her own pace. His hands held her hips, helping her. "You have the worst form of punishment ever. You know that I'm going to start telling you dirty stories every time we get into a vehicle if this is the outcome."

He leaned forward and captured her mouth. They

moved faster and faster. She could feel the sweet release coming. Then he kissed his way to her ear and whispered, "Then maybe I should spank you."

She came. It hit her hard and fast. He kept going until he found his release and she sagged against him.

"I think you should stay at my house," he said as he ran his hand over her hair.

She hid her smile in his shoulder as she said, "I'd like that."

Chapter Fifteen

Sam needed to get a grip. After they'd righted their clothes and refastened their seat belts, he started driving again. Something about Nicole drove him to distraction. When he made love to her, all those doubting and guilty voices in his head quieted, and it was only him and her.

That, and it felt extremely good. He'd thought about ending it when they got home, but then Nicole had spoken and he hadn't wanted to get there. He wanted to keep her to himself for a little bit longer.

As he pulled into the driveway, he saw a familiar car parked near the house. His gut clenched.

"Whose car is that?" Nicole ran her hands over her hair and smoothed her skirt.

"Luke's." He couldn't form an emotion as he spoke, and the word came out flat.

"Were you expecting him?" Nicole clasped her hands together almost gleefully. "When I left, he was so young. I can't wait to meet the man he's grown into."

"He's in a serious relationship." Sam had no idea where that came from.

"I know. You said that a while ago. A girl in his class? I've never heard of her, though. Didn't you say Penny someone?" She turned to face him, obviously not put off by his tone, either not hearing his jealousy or not caring. She was amazing.

"Penny Montgomery. Do you remember Mrs. Montgomery and her antiques shop?" At her nod, he continued, "Penny is her granddaughter."

"This is the girl who kissed you to make Luke break up with her?" She raised one eyebrow.

"Yeah." He put the truck in Park and stared at the car, wondering how long Luke had been here. Had he run into John or the twins taking care of the place? Sam pushed open his door. Before he could even get down, Nicole pushed open her door and jumped down. He had wanted to open the door for her, but Nicole didn't have the patience for that.

She met him in front of the truck. "So, what are we going with here? We're lovers? Friends? Bunk buddies?"

He rolled his eyes and she laughed.

"Are we going to stand outside all day? Because if you wanted, we could wander into the barn and put the backseat of that old clunker you are fixing up to good use." She wiggled her eyebrows in mock suggestion. "I could tell you a few dirty stories, and you could dole out the punishment."

He smiled, but before he could say anything, the screen door slammed shut.

"Holy crap!" Luke said. "Is that a real smile? I didn't think your face could bend that way anymore." Laughter filled Luke's voice, and Sam knew he was only teasing.

It sat wrong with Sam, though, and his smile vanished. "I smile."

"Sometimes your lips twitch that way." Luke came down off the porch and walked to where Sam was. His eyes gave Nicole a once-over in a friendly hey-do-I-know-you kind of way.

"Or just one corner will pop up," Nicole added.

"Exactly." Luke turned his attention to her and held out his hand. "Luke Ward."

"Seriously?" She glanced up at Sam. Her eyes danced in merriment as if to say, "Do you believe this kid?" She brushed Luke's hand aside and went for the kill. The hug. "When I left, you were at least five inches shorter than me. Did they feed you whole cows while I was gone?"

Luke looked at Sam quizzically while Nicole rested her head on Luke's chest. Sam just shook his head and smiled. This was what Nicole did. It was who she was. And he loved that about her.

"Should I know you?" Luke finally asked.

"Should you know me? I'm deeply offended. How many girls beat you up when you threw mud at them? Granted, I pulled my punches so you wouldn't run to your mother and get me in trouble, but you totally deserved every one of those hits to your arm."

"Nikki Baxter?" Luke said incredulously.

She pulled her head off his chest and looked up at him. "I go by Nicole now."

He hugged her back. Though the contact was completely nonsexual, Sam felt it had gone on long enough and cleared his throat.

Nicole glanced over at him and winked before releasing Luke, putting her arm around Sam's waist and leaning into his side. He sighed, not with happiness, but because of what would happen.

Luke's eyes went round. If they had been cartoon eyes, they would have popped out of his head. His gaze darted between the two of them. He opened his mouth and then closed it.

"Where's Penny?" Sam hoped to distract him. He didn't move away from Nicole. She felt too good pressed up against him.

Luke shook himself and said, "She's in town going over the books for the store with Maggie. Brady said you were due back today, so I thought I'd come over and check out the old ticker."

Luke glanced at Nicole for a second as if he were afraid she didn't know and he'd just spilled the beans. Not that what he'd said had been at all informative.

"She knows about my heart," Sam said. "Should we go inside?"

Somehow her knowing about his heart made Luke's eyes even bigger. Sam just shook his head as Luke turned and led them into the kitchen. Luke had a bag with his stethoscope and blood pressure cuff in it.

Sam took his normal seat, and Nicole sat across from him. He could see the curiosity burning in her eyes. She had questions about his heart that she'd never asked him. Or maybe she'd just never found the time to ask him.

Luke listened to Sam's heart first and then took his

blood pressure. "Everything going okay? Keeping your strenuous activity to a minimum?"

Sam grunted his response. He was fine, but if he said that, Doc Luke might make him lie down and take a nap. Though if he could convince Nicole to play nurse…

Luke put the back of his hand against Sam's forehead and Sam automatically backed away. "What are you doing?"

"Checking for fever. You must be delirious with all that smiling. It's not natural." Luke shook his head glumly, but his eyes were crinkled with laughter.

"I'm not smiling now," Sam complained.

Nicole laughed. "I'll let you know if I ever get him to outright laugh. I've caught a few chuckles, but I know somewhere there is a full, rich laugh inside that man, just waiting to get out."

Luke looked at Nicole as if he was trying to dissect her. "What brought you to Tawnee Valley?"

Nicole raised her gaze to Luke. "Downsized, dumped and homeless. Camping out at Dad's until I get back on my feet."

"You were out west somewhere, right?" Luke said.

"California. You guys should have come to visit. It's a whole different world out there." Her green eyes sparkled as her gaze landed on Sam. His heart squeezed.

"No reason to if you aren't there anymore." Luke smiled back and forth at them. If he didn't feel like a third wheel yet, maybe if Sam stared at him long enough, he'd take the hint and leave.

"Where are you staying while you are in town?" Nicole stretched back in the chair, her body taut.

"Penny's house. Near Brady and Maggie's. We're going back and forth between St. Louis and Tawnee

Valley until my residency is finished. You should both join us for dinner tonight at Brady's. We don't often get to eat as a family anymore." Luke's gaze fell on Sam. "What do you say, Sam?"

Nicole looked at him expectantly. She would want him to go and be with his family. She seemed to think that they would accept him with open arms even after all the crap he put them through. Hell, if it got Luke to leave right now...

"I guess we're coming to dinner."

Faking a headache hadn't been an option. So Sam and Nicole sat side by side at Maggie's table once again. This time, both Luke and Penny had joined them. Even though they'd never met before—Nicole had left Tawnee Valley shortly before Penny arrived—the two women were becoming fast friends.

The whole thing seemed very domestic. Sam could almost picture his mother and father and their pride at seeing their family together again. He missed them.

"I have pie if anyone has room." Maggie picked up a couple of plates and lifted her eyebrows.

"I couldn't eat another bite," Brady said as he leaned back in his chair. There was a chorus of similar statements. Maggie just smiled and headed to the kitchen. Penny rose to help.

Nicole covered Sam's hand on the table, and when he turned to her, she gave him a soft smile that went straight to his heart. She grabbed his plate and hers and followed the other women to the kitchen. She was amazing. Amber grabbed Flicker's leash and took him outside.

They could hear the murmurs of talking from the

kitchen and little bursts of laughter as they sat there. Three brothers. Bound together by their parents, torn apart by Sam's need to feel in control of a situation he hadn't been ready for. It was no excuse. It was unforgivable. They should hate him.

They all looked similar enough to be identifiable as brothers, but each of them was a unique blend of their mother and father. Each of them had taken a very different path to end up here with the others.

How had this happened? After everything he'd done, they were here together again. But for how long? How long before Sam hurt one of them again? Or Nicole?

"You and Nicole, huh?" Luke said, addressing the elephant in the room.

Sam didn't meet his eyes and didn't say anything. He knew she was too good for him and this thing between them would be over before it really had a chance. If he didn't sabotage it now, he'd hurt her later, and she'd change. Those soft smiles, those big grins, those dancing eyes would be gone forever because of him.

"I don't think he's going to talk about it." Brady leaned forward with his elbows on the table. "Sam likes to keep to himself."

Didn't they know that everyone was better off when he kept to himself?

"You know, he smiled at least three times when I visited the farm earlier. I think someone is smitten." Luke leaned back his chair, balancing on two of the legs. "I didn't think anyone could—"

"Could what?" Sam leveled his gaze on Luke, who looked amazed that Sam could actually speak. "Could want me? Could love me?"

Luke set down his chair. His face flooded with concern. "That's not what I was going to say. Why would you even think that?"

The room closed in on Sam, and his collar felt tighter than a moment before. His gaze darted to Brady, who had a similar expression of concern on his face.

"Sam, we don't blame you—"

Sam stood so abruptly his chair fell backward. "Why the hell not? Why don't you blame me? Lord knows I blame myself every day. How much happier would you have been, Luke, if I'd been honest about what had happened when Penny kissed me? How can you forgive me for those lost years?"

Luke began, "I don't—"

Sam wasn't listening, though. He was through listening. "And you." He turned to meet Brady's sober expression. "Why don't you hate me? Why do you invite me to your house and pretend that I'm someone who deserves to be your brother? I kept you away from your daughter for eight years. Your daughter! I could have let you know at any point. I could have swallowed my damned pride and told you about Maggie and Amber, but I didn't. And yet you invite me here. Let me be a part of your life, which I don't deserve."

His throat thickened. No one spoke. He glanced toward the kitchen and at the three women standing there. So different, yet the same. He'd let every one of them down.

Their focus wasn't on him, though. It was behind him.

"You kept Daddy away." There was a slight hitch in the words, a disbelief that made Sam want to say it wasn't true.

Amber's words broke Sam's heart, and tears welled

in his eyes as he turned to face the person he'd done the most unforgivable thing to. The person who had pulled him into her world even as he tried to push away. The person who had believed in him, even though he'd done nothing to make her.

Amber's eyes flowed over with tears. She stood there and stared at him with his mother's eyes. So disillusioned.

He wanted to say something to make it okay. Instead, a single tear slipped down his cheek. He couldn't say anything to take away the hurt and pain he'd caused her. No words would ever make his actions right.

He nodded his head, acknowledging his guilt.

Her lip trembled and she shook her head violently. "No."

"Amber…" Maggie took a few steps into the dining room, her hands outstretched for her daughter.

Amber backed up a step, still staring at Sam. Her face was a younger version of his mother's, and all the self-doubt and self-blame he'd had came rushing forward. In disappointing his niece, he'd disappointed his mother.

Amber raced up the steps and slammed her bedroom door behind her. Maggie and Brady both headed for the hallway. Maggie put her hand on Brady's arm and went upstairs alone.

Sam couldn't look at any of them. This was what he'd wanted. This was what he deserved. He walked out the front door, needing air, needing to fill his lungs. To fill the ache in his chest and the burning in his gut.

A hand slipped into his from behind and he turned to see Nicole move beside him.

"Let's go home," she said.

The word echoed in Sam's head, bringing with it the memory he'd tried to forget for the past nine years.

Brady stood in front of him, angry and wanting to leave. Sitting at the kitchen table, Sam was frustrated with Brady's selfishness. Brady had been the one to get to go away to college. He hadn't had to try to figure out how to raise an angry, grieving teenage boy. He didn't have to go through every day feeling as if any minute, Dad would walk around the corner or Mom would smile when he came into the kitchen. Brady had escaped, leaving Sam to deal with the mess.

"Home?" Brady spit out the word as if it left a bad taste in his mouth.

"Like Dad always wanted. Like Mom wanted. The three of us together."

"This isn't home."

The words rang in Sam's ears, burning through his heart. He rose, his hands balling into fists. He looked down at Brady, willing him to take it back.

But Brady didn't back down. "God, Sam, have you deluded yourself that much? This can't be home, because home is Mom and Dad. Home was an illusion we had as kids. A safety net to keep us protected. Now? Home is shattered all around us."

Rage shook through Sam. How dare he? Didn't he have any loyalty? Any sense of responsibility? "Stop it."

"Luke is a mess. You are a mess. I'm a freaking mess. We don't belong anywhere. You can't keep trying to bind us to this place. We don't belong together."

Sam turned back to watch Luke and Brady through the door. Brady had left for his internship in England after that argument. It had been after Luke's high school graduation. After Penny had kissed Sam. Luke had barely spoken to Sam, even though he'd come back to help during summers. In four short years, Sam had lost both his parents and his brothers.

You are a mess. And Sam had never gotten better. He hadn't fixed what was broken.

We don't belong together. No, Luke and Brady belonged together. Family was important. Just Sam didn't belong with anyone. He dropped his head and let Nicole lead him away.

Chapter Sixteen

Nicole opened the door to the farmhouse and went inside. Sam followed her. He hadn't said anything since they'd left Brady's. She wrung her hands, not knowing what to say or to do. She spun and put her arms around him.

He closed his arms around her loosely, but it was as if all the fight had left him.

"Do you want something to drink?" she asked, trying for some semblance of normalcy.

"No."

At least it was a word.

She lifted her face to look at him. His eyes were tired, and he looked as if the whole world was weighing him down. She wanted to say she loved him. To kiss him and make it all better. But he seemed so far away right now. So closed off. In a place where she couldn't reach him. Her heart clattered to a stop in her chest.

Shaking it off, she said, "Let's go to bed."

She led the way once again. There was no way to fix this. It should have never come out, but it was there now. All the pain and guilt and remorse that Sam had tucked away were now an open festering wound.

She wanted to heal him. She wanted him to know that she still loved him and that it mattered. He mattered.

When they reached his bedroom, she undressed down to her underwear and then helped him out of his clothes. He was numb and almost vacant. His silence gnawed at her. Time should help. Amber just needed time. He just needed time.

She helped him into the bed and then climbed in next to him. She cuddled with him, lying in the crook of his arm, her arm draped across him.

All the words she had failed her. She couldn't say it was going to be okay. She couldn't say that Amber would get over it. She wanted so badly to give him that reassurance, but she couldn't.

"I love you, Sam." If they were the only words left on earth, they still couldn't express what she felt for him. How deeply those emotions touched her.

When she reached up to stroke his cheek, her hand met the wetness there. She leaned up and moved so that she could see his face and the silent tears falling there.

"I'm here, Sam." She kissed his lips, not passionately, but tenderly, trying to let him know with her touch that she was here with him and that she wasn't going anywhere, but not sure that her words or touch were getting through. "I'm not going anywhere."

His eyes met hers and held her captivated. Deep inside her, the words echoed through her like a death knell: *he's letting me go.*

She lowered her mouth to his and kissed him, trying to prove to him that she loved him and that she wouldn't leave. He held all the cards. He would deal them however he felt was right, but that didn't mean she'd go out without making him know how much she loved him.

His hands moved to cradle her head. This wasn't goodbye sex. She wouldn't let it be. She couldn't let it be. She didn't want to go to Atlanta by herself. She didn't want to go anywhere that Sam wasn't.

All the fears of finding a job that suited her swept out of her. She'd fallen into accounting in college because nothing else had seemed like a good fit. She'd fallen into a relationship with Jeremy because it was good enough. Ever since she was fourteen, she'd never felt as if she fit in or that anywhere was home, because this was her home. In Sam's arms in the middle of nowhere, Illinois.

She wanted to run outside and scream it at the crickets and owls. To those two lonesome coyotes.

Sam rolled her to her back, and she showed him with her mouth and hands and arms how much she loved him. Even though every touch he gave her seemed to whisper goodbye, she wouldn't hear it. She wanted to bask in love for as long as she could. She wanted to be his forever.

There had to be a way.

Through the window, Sam watched the lightening sky. Nicole slept soundly against his chest, and he held her tight within his arms. Waking up with her filled him with immeasurable joy, but she needed to get on with her life without him. It was the right thing to do.

It left him feeling hollowed out. He'd ruined everything. The one thing he could do was keep the farm his parents had trusted him with and pass it on to one of Brady's or Luke's kids.

Sam wasn't suited for the world outside of this farm. He loved farming. Staying here with all the memories and disappointments echoing in every structure was his cross to bear. He didn't deserve happiness.

The look on Amber's face had been the kick that he needed. He'd reached too high. Wanted too much. It wasn't his to have. Nicole wasn't his to have. He couldn't start over.

Nicole stirred in his arms. She lifted her head and smiled at him as if nothing had happened. As if everything would be sunshine and daisies and the world was a fabulous place. He'd miss her smiles.

"Good morning." She stretched and looked at the clock on the nightstand. "Time to make the donuts?"

His brows drew together. "Donuts?"

"Like that Dunkin' Donuts commercial." She propped her chin on her hands on his chest. "Chores and then breakfast or breakfast and then chores."

A tightness formed in his chest when he thought of how often Amber had helped him with the chores. He'd given her only the little things to do. Things he knew she'd enjoy, like feeding the baby animals.

He slid out from under Nicole and rolled to the side, sitting on the edge of the bed. His body, where she'd been only a moment before, felt cold. He took in a deep breath.

"Are you thinking about what happened last night?"

Nicole moved behind him. He could feel her weight shifting the mattress, and then she stood. Her feet padded around his bed until she stood in front of him. One of his T-shirts covered her down to her midthigh.

He gave a short nod. She wouldn't offer forgiveness. It was one of the things he loved the most about Nicole. She accepted him for the screwed-up guy he was, but he wasn't right for her.

"She'll get over it, Sam. Maybe not today or in a week, but over time, she will understand why you did it."

"No, she won't." He lifted his head so he could see her green eyes. Watch the light die from them. "I won't get over it. How is she supposed to understand when I don't understand?"

She sat next to him on the bed and took his hand. "You're family. That's what matters."

"I don't deserve to be forgiven."

She was quiet for a moment, as if she was trying to find the right words. There were no "right" words, though. "Remember when I left for California? Do you remember that day?"

He nodded his head.

"We'd spent an hour out in the tree house, hoping that if they couldn't find me, I wouldn't have to go." Her hair fell like a curtain around her face when she leaned forward, but he could see the small, sad smile hiding beneath. "I was so angry at my dad. If I'd been asked where I wanted to be, I would have stayed, but I felt like he hadn't wanted me. Because I was the girl. He kept the twins, but not me."

She tipped her face his way and tucked her hair behind her ears. "When it came down to it, though, I realized that Mom needed me. Dad knew that. The twins stayed behind because she couldn't take care of us all, but she deserved one of her children. Eventually the ache went away, and I realized how hard it was to get that far across the country for a visit. I'm not saying it was only a day or that I came to this realization suddenly, but eventually I forgave him. I know he loves me and he missed me. And even though it hurt for quite some time, I got over it."

"I didn't have a noble reason for keeping Brady away." Sam felt so small, as if he was eight years old and had just gotten in trouble for shoving Luke out of the way when Luke had tried to play with him. "At the time, I thought that I was doing it to protect Brady. To give him a chance at the life he wanted."

She squeezed his hand.

He looked her in the eyes and confessed, "I was angry at him. He had everything. He'd been able to go to college. He'd been free to make the decision to take an internship overseas. He made something of himself that had nothing to do with this farm. And I hated him for it."

He waited for her faith in him to leave her eyes. But she just sat with him. She didn't yell at him for being an ass. He didn't deserve her faith.

He scrubbed his hand down his face and looked up at the ceiling. Somewhere he had the strength to tell her to go. To make that light for him die in her eyes. But he felt so bruised right now that he couldn't even lash out.

"I've got to work." He stood and went to his drawers, pulling out his clothes and jerking them on.

Nicole's arms went around him, and she pressed her

body and cheek against his back. He pulled her arms from him and turned.

"Why do you do that?"

She shrugged. "I do what I feel."

"Maybe that's why you have so many issues with guys. Maybe you smother them with too much attention. Sometimes people want to be alone with their thoughts and emotions. Not everything needs to be dragged out and inspected under a microscope."

She pressed her lips into a thin line. "Do you want to be alone?"

"Yes. Yes. Yes. How many times are you going to ignore me and do what you want, instead of what I need? I don't want you here. I want to be alone."

For a moment he thought she might cry, but she blinked a couple times and then reached down to grab her clothes. He wanted to reach out to her, but he stopped himself. It would be easier this way.

At the doorway to his bedroom, she turned and looked him in the eye. Her green eyes were brimming with tears. "You know, you can try to break my heart. You can try to say goodbye. You can say that you don't want me, don't need me, don't love me." She drew in a deep breath and straightened her shoulders. "But if there's anything you should know, Sam Ward, it's that I know you. So lash out all you want, but when you are ready, I'll be where I've always been. Waiting for you."

He didn't say anything as she turned and left him alone.

Chapter Seventeen

Nicole stepped over the fence and passed the tree house. It had been a week since she'd left Sam's house. She'd been certain that when he finally calmed down, he'd call. Well, that was one thing she no longer had the luxury to wait for.

She glanced at the house but headed for the barn. Strains of Def Leppard could be heard coming through the open door. She wound her way through the old barn to the garage. All she could see were his feet peeking out from under the car.

On a workbench, an old black boom box cranked out tunes at a ridiculous volume. She pressed Pause, and the room went silent with the exception of the clunk under the car, followed by a muffled curse.

Sam rolled out from under the car and stood. His eyes sought the cause of the sudden silence and landed on her.

"Hey," she said, leaning against the workbench as if she had every right to be there. She'd worn a pair of shorts and a bright T-shirt that made her feel good about her body. She needed everything in her arsenal to get through this.

"Hey," he said back. He wiped his hands on a rag but didn't move from his spot next to the car.

"Making any progress on the car?" She pointed and would have slapped herself on the forehead for doing so, but everything felt so awkward right now. She'd been in his arms a week ago. He'd taken her to new heights in the bedroom. She'd confessed her love for him.

And he'd thrown her away like yesterday's leftovers.

"It'll run eventually." He put his hands in his pockets.

"I just came over to tell you I got the job in Atlanta." She watched for a reaction, any reaction. Happy, sad, indifferent.

"I knew you would."

This was harder than she thought it would be. She slid a finger through the dirt on the boom box. "I don't have to go, you know. I could stay…"

He leaned against the car. All nonchalant six-foot-something of him. "For what?"

"For you. For me. For us." She needed to put it all out there. This could be her only shot. She had to make a decision between waiting for this man to come to the realization that he loved her, or taking a job and starting her life over.

"Why would you do that? What good would that do?" His eyes revealed nothing. But she'd felt the connection between them. She knew deep inside that he felt it, too.

"I love you, Sam."

"Words. That's all that is. You'll get over it. I need to

honor my parents' wishes and keep my farm. You need to find your own life. One that doesn't include me." He turned his back to her and walked over to a workbench.

She straightened. "You don't mean that."

He slammed down the wrench on the workbench, the metal ringing through the small space. "Yes, I do." He spun and stalked toward her. "I will screw up your life just like I screwed up Brady's and Luke's."

She didn't back down as he came closer. "You can't screw up my life, because it's mine. I'm the only one who can screw it up."

"And that's all you've done with it is screw it up. You want to give up a job that will pay good money and put you back on the track you'd set out for yourself to do what? Stay with me?"

She poked her finger in his chest. "It was never my life. It was my mom's ideal life. I followed it because it was safe."

"I'm not safe." With him towering over her in his anger, she could almost believe those words.

"I'm done with safe. I'm done being someone else's puppet. I'm done waiting for life to come and tell me what to do. I want to be with you. I want to share my life with you because I love you. I always have."

His voice was cold when he said, "I know. You wrote it all in those letters to me."

The air left the room and she felt ill. "You read…"

She covered her mouth as the horror filled her with a sick, oozing feeling.

"Your little love notes to me?"

She shook her head. She'd started those as real letters to Sam, but over time, when she didn't send them, she'd used him as her diary, telling him things she wouldn't have shared with anyone else. Now he knew everything she'd felt since she'd left him, and she knew hardly anything about him.

He got a glint in his eyes, and that familiar spark of desire raced through her. He leaned in until they were so close, she could feel his breath against her lips. "How do you think I knew your fantasies?"

She opened her mouth and closed it. He was trying to push her away. The problem was, it was working. This wasn't the guy she'd fallen for. This was the bitter man he'd become. If she hadn't known that guy still existed, she would have run screaming.

She stared into his eyes, not moving away, but not leaning closer. "If you keep pushing people away, Sam Ward, you'll be alone forever."

"Good." He hesitated a moment, long enough for her almost to feel the kiss that was waiting right there for them. That moment of softness as his eyes flickered over her lips. But the moment passed, and he backed away.

"You don't mean that," she said.

"Run home, Nikki."

Sam slammed the door as he went into the house. He wanted to break something. He needed to destroy something the way he'd destroyed Nicole. It was for the best, his mind kept saying, like a CD stuck on repeat. It hadn't felt right.

His chest ached, and he rubbed at the muscle there, but it didn't help. It had felt as if a sickly ooze was running over his body as he'd tried to make her believe he didn't want her anymore. He slammed his hand against the counter.

A car pulled down the drive. Sam walked over to the window and pulled the curtain aside to see who it was. Probably John Baxter to beat him up for upsetting his only daughter. He'd love to have someone punch him right now. He deserved it.

The car wasn't John's, though. It was Maggie Ward's.

Maggie slid out of the driver's seat and turned to the backseat to talk with Amber. After a minute, she closed her door and headed for the house.

She didn't bother to knock. No one ever did, except Nicole. As she stepped into the kitchen, she turned to Sam. "Amber wanted to come out and talk to you."

"Why? So I can ruin Santa, too?" He didn't feel up to any more damage today. He already felt bad enough.

"No, she needs to talk to you, and you need to talk to her." Maggie slipped outside before Sam could tell her no again.

Sam dropped into his kitchen chair. Even his dogs wouldn't hang out with him in his current mood. What could he do for his niece, who knew the truth, who knew he'd failed her when she'd needed him most? He put his head in his hands.

"Uncle Sam?"

He made a sound so she'd know where he was, but he didn't want to climb out of his remorse.

A chair scraped against the floor. Amber inhaled a breath before saying, "I was very angry the other day."

As you should have been.

"But I shouldn't have been."

He lifted his head and looked into his niece's eyes. She sat next to him at the table.

"I could have missed my daddy for eight years, but I had my grandma and mom and Penny. I wondered about him, but I was loved without him." She set her hands on the table. "Mom said you told her about Dad not knowing, so she could go and tell him. She said that you made sure we were taken care of before that. Daddy said that he wishes he'd been with me my whole life, but that we have each other now and we should be happy that we have what we have. I guess what I'm trying to say is, I forgive you."

For a moment he was dumbfounded. He couldn't even forgive himself. "How?"

She narrowed her eyes at him. "You are sorry, aren't you?"

"Yes."

"And you promise never to do anything like it again, right?"

"Not in a million years."

"See." She smiled. "Then it's all better. I have my daddy now, thanks to you. I also have my uncle Luke and I have you. Don't tell Uncle Luke, but you are my favorite uncle."

He swallowed the lump in his throat. "But what if I don't forgive myself?"

"Well, that's just silly. Everyone makes mistakes. If we didn't make mistakes, we wouldn't grow. That's what Nana always used to say. I think it means that mistakes happen and we should learn from them or something." She shrugged. "Is someone still sad because of it?"

He thought of Brady and Maggie, and Luke and Penny, and their lives together. No matter how they got there, they seemed to have made it out all right. Something Nicole said came back to haunt him. *So willing to take the blame for your actions. Would you take a little credit?* "You're pretty smart for a kid."

"I know." Amber grinned and leaned back in her chair. "Are you going to ask Nicole to marry you?"

Sam cringed. "I think it's a little late for that."

"Why? She was talking to Penny yesterday about possibly helping with the store."

That was before he'd made a giant ass of himself and before Atlanta had come calling. "I don't think she'll forgive me."

"Do you want me to talk to her for you?" Amber patted his hand.

He shook his head. "I think this one I have to do myself."

"Just tell her you're sorry and will never do it again. And then don't do it again."

Nicole had seen Sam's truck parked outside the shop at least two other times this week. She was tempted to walk out there and beat on the window, but she held back. After all, he wanted to be alone. He could be alone in his stupid truck.

Penny's antiques shop, What Goes Around Comes Around, was just the distraction Nicole had needed. While Maggie had been doing a pretty decent job of working there, she needed to be home in the afternoons when Amber got out of school. Both Maggie and Penny had been there for her when Nicole had called to complain about Sam. She'd never really had a girls' night before. They'd ordered pizza and put on a chick flick and told her she was too good for him anyway.

It hadn't made her want him less, but it'd felt good to vent. If she were too good for him, why wasn't he with her? Her father was keen to keep her at home now that she was back. When she'd told him she turned down the Atlanta job and wanted to stay, he'd pulled her into a tight hug. And she knew she'd made the right decision.

It wasn't just Sam who had been without his family for years. She wanted to get to know her father and brothers again. And at some point, Sam would come to his senses and realize that she was the only one for him. She just hoped it would be before she was old and gray.

The door bell jingled, and she lifted her head from the numbers she'd been staring at. Sam stood in the doorway, looking incredibly uncomfortable. Good. And also incredibly handsome. He was freshly shaven, with his good jeans and a newer shirt on.

She pressed her lips together and stared down at the numbers as they blurred in front of her eyes. She refused to let him see her cry, but this position made it hard to hold the tears in.

"Hey," he said and moved to stand on the other side of the counter from her.

Taking a deep breath, she lifted her eyes and stared at him.

"I see you haven't left for Atlanta yet," he said.

"Nope." There was no way she would make this easy on him.

He pushed his hand through his hair. "I'm not selling the farm."

"Good." She crossed her arms, trying not to give away how much she wanted to hug him, to kiss him. She needed to stay strong.

"I…" He stopped.

Nicole couldn't hold back anymore. "Look. I can't be with you. I can't do this anymore. I know you are a good man, but I can't spend the rest of my life trying to convince you of that. I need to find my own life. Figure out what I want."

She nodded and recrossed her arms. There, she'd said it.

"Nicole, I'm glad for you. I want you to be happy. I just wanted to tell you…" He ducked his head before lifting his eyes back to hers. "I'm sorry. I've been an ass."

"Yes, you have."

"You are one of the best things I've ever had in my life, and I threw you away because I was afraid."

Her arms loosened a little. "That's right."

He took a step toward the end of the counter. "I was afraid that I would end up hurting you because I've always hurt the ones I love."

"You hurt me." She nodded before fully digesting his statement.

"I did." He took another step and rounded the counter, trapping her near the cash register. "I didn't want to, but I knew it would only be a matter of time before you discovered the truth."

"The truth?" Her heartbeat had quickened with each step that brought him closer to her.

"That I love you and never want you to leave me ever again."

Tears welled in her eyes as a small smile formed on her lips. "You do?"

"I've been lost since I was fourteen because the only person who ever made me feel whole left me. I don't want to feel that way again. I want you to come home with me and stay there forever. Grow old with me and have a half-dozen children to love. Be part of my life and save me from myself when I try to do something wrong again. Stop waiting for good enough and be loved by me with everything I have to give. I will never try to push you away again."

She covered the shaky grin that grew on her lips. Tears spilled down her cheeks unchecked. "What exactly are you asking me, Sam?"

"Stay with me, Nicole. Live in my house. Eat my food—"

"Only if I prepare it."

He closed the remaining distance until a hairbreadth parted them. "Sleep in my bed. Love me and let me love you. Make me the happiest man. Will you marry me?"

"Say it again," she whispered. Happiness welled in her heart so much that she could have flown if he'd asked her to.

"The whole thing?" He lifted his hand to cup her cheek and brush away her tears with his thumb.

"No." She shook her head. "Just the love thing."

He brought his head down until their foreheads touched. His dark blue eyes were filled with emotion. "I love you, Nicole."

She placed her hands on his chest. "I'm sorry, I didn't quite hear that. Could you say it louder?"

"I love you." And then it happened. Right there, Sam Ward laughed. She'd been right. It was dark and rich and made all her nerve endings stand up and her insides pulse happily.

"Are you sure you aren't ill?" She held her hand to his forehead.

"I love you and want to marry you. If you'll have me." He kissed her, a slow kiss filled with promise.

"I don't know. I was pretty mad." She waited while he kissed her again, this time pulling her into his arms.

"Marry me," he whispered against her lips.

"I love you, Sam. Yes, I'll marry you."

He lifted her from the ground and spun her around in his arms before settling back into a kiss that was definitely not workplace appropriate.

A discrete cough pulled him away from her, and they both turned to see Bitsy Clemons, the town busybody, standing on the other side of the counter. Sam released her, and they both straightened themselves.

Bitsy smiled a devious little smile. "What's this I hear about a wedding?"

Nicole looked up at Sam and could see the resignation in his eyes. Before nightfall, everyone in Tawnee Valley was going to know that Sam and Nicole had been caught kissing and were engaged. But when he smiled at her, she knew it didn't matter. What mattered was that, even though years and miles had kept them apart, they'd finally found each other. Together, they could do anything.

Epilogue

Christmas

Sam brushed the snow off his boots before opening the kitchen door. The whole house smelled of roasted ham. The kitchen was filled with Maggie, Penny and Nicole. All of them were working on something, pulling out pots and pans that his mother had always used for the holidays. Pride welled within him.

Penny's mother, Cheryl, was even here standing at the sink, trying to keep up with the dishes.

"Get out of the doorway. It's cold out here," Luke said.

Sam moved, and Brady and Luke came through the door with a small mass between them covered in snow and a purple snowsuit. Amber started taking off her boots, and the brothers followed suit.

"Try to make sure to put them on the rug this time,"

Nicole called over her shoulder. "If my socks get wet stepping in your puddles…"

Sam dropped his winter gear on the drying rack and walked over into the mess of women trying to get dinner ready. He put his arms around Nicole from behind, and she squeaked.

"I'm busy." Her voice held a smile, though.

He kissed her neck. "Can't a man kiss his wife?"

"Only if he does it nicely."

He straightened. "You were the one who put snow down my back yesterday."

"Yes, but it isn't nice to put snow down pregnant women's backs."

He smiled. "You are going to milk this for the remaining six months, aren't you?"

"Only six months? Honey, I'm going to milk this for the rest of my life." Nicole turned and kissed him.

Amber ran past to her mother, Maggie, and put her hands on Maggie's expanded belly. "Is my sister kicking?"

"Not right now." Maggie smoothed her hand over Amber's dark hair. "Maybe after we unwrap gifts, she'll be up to kicking again."

Brady joined his family and gave Maggie a kiss. "Come on, Amber. You can help me set the table. Your grandma always used her blue plates for Christmas."

Luke went over to Penny and pulled her into his arms. Unlike the sweet peck that Brady and Maggie had shared, Luke gave Penny a kiss that had her unbalanced when they came up for air.

"Newlyweds," Sam said and rolled his eyes.

Nicole swatted him on the arm playfully. "Just because we got a honeymoon baby doesn't mean we aren't still newlyweds."

"Go sit in the other room so we can finish getting things ready," Penny said, pointing the way for Luke. "You, too, Sam. We have enough to do without tripping over you two."

"Yes, ma'am." Sam followed Luke into the living room, where Brady was already sitting. The room was far from drab now that Nicole was living here. She'd brightened everything from the walls to the curtains and the furniture. The TV was on low as the Christmas parade went by on the screen.

The tree was in the corner, decorated just as their mother would have decorated it, including a few new pieces from every one of the families. Lights trimmed the house, too. It had been years since the holidays had seemed this festive.

Amber ran into the room and squeezed onto the couch next to Sam. Her eyes kept darting to all the presents under the tree.

"Mom would have been proud, seeing those three in her kitchen," Brady said, rocking back in his chair.

"Dad would have flipped a bit if he saw how much Sam spent on that new combine." Luke grinned at the TV.

Thinking about his parents didn't hurt as much now. Sam would always miss them. They were a huge part of him. But he had a family again, including his brothers and their wives, his niece and his almost-niece, and soon his own child. And Nicole, the one person who had healed his heart. His life was full, and his heart had never felt more whole.

He breathed deeply and let it out. "I think we did all right."

* * * * *

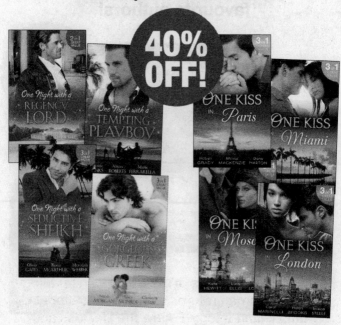

MILLS & BOON®

Why not subscribe?
Never miss a title and save money too!

Here's what's available to you if you join the exclusive **Mills & Boon Book Club** today:

- ✦ *Titles up to a month ahead of the shops*
- ✦ *Amazing discounts*
- ✦ *Free P&P*
- ✦ *Earn Bonus Book points that can be redeemed against other titles and gifts*
- ✦ *Choose from monthly or pre-paid plans*

Still want more?
Well, if you join today we'll even give you
50% OFF your first parcel!

So visit **www.millsandboon.co.uk/subs**
or call Customer Relations on **020 8288 2888**
to be a part of this exclusive Book Club!

MILLS & BOON®

Cherish™

EXPERIENCE THE ULTIMATE RUSH OF FALLING IN LOVE